mary-kateandashley

so little time

Check out these great

so little time

titles:

Book 1: **how to train a boy**

Book 2: **instant boyfriend**

Book 3: **too good to be true**

Book 4: **just between us**

Book 5: **tell me about it**

Book 6: **secret crush**

Coming Soon!

Book 7: **girl talk**

Book 8: **the love factor**

mary-kateandashley
so little time

tell me about it

By Nancy Butcher

Based on the teleplay by Marcy Vosburgh

HarperCollins*Entertainment*

An Imprint of HarperCollinsPublishers

A PARACHUTE PRESS BOOK

A PARACHUTE PRESS BOOK

Parachute Publishing, L.L.C.
156 Fifth Avenue
Suite 325
NEW YORK
NY 10010

First published in the USA by HarperEntertainment 1999
First published in Great Britain by HarperCollins*Entertainment* 2002
HarperCollins*Entertainment* is an imprint of HarperCollins*Publishers* Ltd,
77-85 Fulham Palace Road, Hammersmith, London W6 8JB

SO LITTLE TIME, characters, names and all related indicia are trademarks of
and © Dualstar Entertainment Group, LLC.
SO LITTLE TIME books created and produced by Parachute Press, L.L.C., in
cooperation with Dualstar Publications, a division of Dualstar Entertainment
Group, LLC.

The HarperCollins website address is
www.fireandwater.com

1 3 5 7 9 8 6 4 2

The authors assert the moral right to be
identified as the authors of the work.

ISBN 0 00 714451 2

Printed and bound in Great Britain by Clays Ltd, St Ives plc

chapter
one

"It's official," fourteen-year-old Chloe Carlson declared to her twin sister. "Today definitely made number one on my top ten list of most horrible Mondays ever!"

Riley Carlson pushed her long straight hair out of her face. "Today wasn't *that* bad, was it?" she asked.

"Are you kidding?" Chloe rolled her eyes. "First we had three major tests in a row. Then the cafeteria ran out of salads and we had to eat mystery meat. Then I broke a nail trying to open my locker. And now this."

"Now what?" Riley glanced around.

The two of them were standing in the doorway of California Dream, their favourite after-school hangout. The place was crowded, but there were still plenty of tables open.

"Our favourite table," Chloe started to explain. She gazed at the booth where they usually sat. It had

1

a great view of Malibu Beach and the ocean. And it was taken!

"Oh, give me a break," Riley said, moving towards an empty table across the room. But before they reached it, the boy sitting in their booth stood up.

"Sorry," he said quickly. He gathered up his soda and fries. "I'll move. I didn't mean to take your spot."

"Wow," Riley said softly. "That was nice. Who's he?"

"I don't know," Chloe admitted. "Some guy from school?"

"I guess so," Riley said as the two of them sat down.

"That was weird," Chloe said. "We don't even know that guy. I mean, sure – we sit at this table every day. But how did *he* know? Are we getting to be *that* predictable?"

"I hope not," Riley said. "Maybe it just means this day isn't going to be such a disaster after all."

Chloe nodded. "You could be right." She picked up the menu that was leaning against the napkin holder on the table. "Let's see." She tried to decide what to order. "I need something to cheer me up. Maybe a malt."

The waitress approached their table with a tray in her hands.

"Hi," she said. "Here you go – a decaf latte for you." She set the steaming mug in front of Riley. "And a lemonade spritzer for you." She put the glass down beside Chloe. "I'll be right back with your bagel to share."

"Wait!" Chloe called. It was too late. The waitress had already spun around and was hurrying back to the counter. She didn't hear Chloe over the music on the jukebox.

"Wow," Riley said, staring at the drinks in front of them. "What's up with that?"

"I don't know," Chloe said. "But we *have* ordered the same exact thing every day for the past month."

"Oh, boy," Riley said. "We *are* totally predictable!"

[Chloe: **What's so wrong with that, you ask? Well, if I'm not careful, I'll turn into someone totally boring, like Marla Ciannelli. She was a girl in my third-grade class. Every Monday she wore her red plaid jumper and white ruffled blouse. On Tuesdays she wore black corduroys and her blue-green sweater. On Wednesdays it was overalls with a yellow T-shirt. On Thursdays... well, you get the point. Anyway, that's my worst nightmare – a life full of boring, boring, boring. Everything the same. At least when it comes to fashion, I've pretty much got it covered – don't I? Hold on. Didn't I wear this cute little green tank top and these lime-green hip huggers last Monday, too? Help!]**

"Hello, Chloe? Earth to Chloe," Riley said.

Chloe started. "What? Did I miss something?"

"Yes. I just asked you what we're going to do this weekend," Riley replied.

"How should I know?" Chloe sighed. "You're the

3

one with the ready-made social life. You're the one with the boyfriend, remember?"

Alex Zimmer was Riley's guy these days. He was a really cute freshman at West Malibu High. He was also a member of a cool band called The Wave. Riley's best friend Sierra Pomeroy was in the band, too.

"Yeah. I know what I'm doing on Saturday," Riley said. "But Alex always hangs out with his buddies on Friday night. How about you? Any plans?"

"Nothing," Chloe said. "Since I dumped Travis, my life has been one big social zero."

Travis was the cute bad-boy Chloe had a crush on – until she found out that he wasn't really interested in anyone but himself.

"So you know what this means," Riley said.

"Oh, no, don't tell me!" Chloe covered her face with her hands. "Not another Friday night with Mom!"

"It's our mother-daughter tradition," Riley joked, using the same voice their mom would use.

"Riley, traditions are for *other* people. Like for remote rainforest tribes where they don't have malls to hang out in," Chloe complained. "We need some spice in our lives."

"Huh?" Riley said.

"Think about it," Chloe said. "All over Malibu, kids our age are going out on dates, going to parties, or hanging out in the mall on Friday night. What are *we* doing?"

"The same thing we've done every Friday night since we were eight?" Riley said.

"Exactly!" Chloe moaned. "Dinner with Mom at the Siam Palace. We'll have one pad thai, one yum yai, and one yum kai."

"Then we'll see a movie," Riley said, picking up the story. "We'll have one large tub-o'-corn, one diet mega-gulp, and one giant box of Mike and Ikes."

"Right," Chloe said. "And then afterwards, we'll go to the ice-cream shop. I'll get the mud pie. You'll get the root-beer float."

"And Mom will sample all the ice-cream flavours with that stupid little pink spoon," Riley reminded her.

Exactly, Chloe thought. It was all so totally predictable! So boring! So Marla Ciannelli!

"Oh, Riley, what are we going to do?" Chloe moaned. "We're in a rut! A big, stupid, endless rut! How are we ever going to get out of it?"

Riley's eyes lit up. "I know! What if I get the mud pie and *you* get the root-beer float?" she suggested.

"Very funny," Chloe said. "Come on, I'm serious. This is an emergency!"

Riley took a sip of her decaf latte just as the waitress brought their sliced bagel.

Chloe reached for the top half.

"Careful," Riley cautioned her. "You *always* take the top half."

That's true! Chloe thought. I do! She dropped the bagel back on the plate.

"Okay, from now on, it's no more bagels after school," Chloe declared. "And we're going to figure out something to do this weekend. Something exciting."

"Like what?" Riley asked.

"Like…" Chloe tried to think of something good. But she couldn't concentrate. Someone behind her was talking, and she couldn't help it, she was listening in on the conversation.

It sounded like they were talking about a party. A totally hip, totally cool party.

That's just what we need! Chloe thought.

"Earth to Chloe," Riley said again.

"Shh!" Chloe leaned forward but motioned with her head to the booth behind her. "Who's sitting back there?" she whispered.

"It's Andrea Ripner," Riley answered super-softly. "She's with Darcy Steiner and two older guys."

Andrea Ripner?

She's so cool! Chloe thought. Andrea was a freshman, like Chloe and Riley, and her clothes were really cute and trendy. She was in Chloe's maths class.

But that's where the similarity stopped. For one thing, Andrea had been a dancer in a music video last summer. For a few months after that, she was on MTV every three hours!

Andrea had beautiful long straight brown hair. All the guys liked her, and she knew it.

Chloe leaned back so she could eavesdrop some more. It wasn't hard to hear Andrea now that the music on the jukebox had changed to a quieter song.

"So who's playing?" Andrea asked one of the guys.

"Double Take," the guy answered. "And two other bands from the valley. It's going to be awesome this week."

"Three bands?" Andrea sounded amazed.

"There's always at least *one* band," the guy said.

"And they have this party every Saturday night?" Andrea said.

"Don't tell me you haven't heard of it!" the guy mocked her. "The Train Wreck is legendary. Man, you freshmen don't know anything, do you?"

"I know how to *not* get caught cutting study hall," Andrea teased him. "Unlike *some* people at this table."

"Ooh, she's got you now, Dan," someone else at the table said.

"We aren't talking about that," Dan said. "Not if you want to come to the Train Wreck."

"So why is it called the Train Wreck, anyway?" Andrea asked.

"It used to be held in a warehouse near the train tracks," Dan explained. "And the name just stuck."

"And besides, you come home every weekend wrecked, right?" Andrea added.

Everyone at the table laughed.

Dan? Chloe thought. Was that Dan Harrington sitting right behind her? He was one of the most popular guys in the senior class.

That's what makes Andrea so cool, Chloe thought. Even though she was Chloe's age, she hung out with a bunch of popular juniors and seniors.

Chloe tried to turn and look without getting caught. Like she was just casually glancing towards the door or trying to spot the waitress or something.

Yes. That was Dan Harrington sitting there!

Chloe strained to hear more.

"So fill her in, dude," the other guy was saying to Dan.

"The party's been going on for about five years," Dan said. "Some guy named P.T. started it before I was a freshman, and now I'm the party-meister. It moves to a different warehouse every week."

"Except when we have it in Guido's Garage," the other guy explained.

"Seriously? You have it in an auto body shop?" Andrea asked. "That's cool!"

Dan laughed and mumbled something Chloe couldn't make out. Then the whole group got up from their booth to leave.

Chloe waited until they were gone before reaching across the table and grabbing her sister's hand.

"That's it!" she said, her eyes glowing with excitement. "That's what we need to do to get out of our rut!"

"What?" Riley asked. "Have a party in a garage?"

"No!" Chloe declared. "Get invited to the Train Wreck!"

"Wow." Riley nodded. "That would be different. But how are we going to do that?"

"I don't know. We've got to think of something," Chloe said.

"Hey, look." Riley stood up and walked to the table where Andrea and Dan had been sitting. "They left something."

Chloe spun around. "What?" She jumped up to see.

"These flyers," Riley said.

A stack of yellow papers was sitting there. Andrea had left them on the table by her seat.

Chloe picked one up. It said:

TRAIN WRECK – Saturday as usual
Be there or have a totally outrageous excuse
for missing it!
(Can you say THREE BANDS???
Can you say dance till you drop??)
All the usual stuff to eat and drink.
Where?? To be determined, as usual!
To find out, ask Rafe the usual question!

"Okay," Chloe said, getting serious. "So now all we have to do is figure out two things. Who's Rafe? And just exactly *what* is the usual question?"

9

chapter two

Riley thought about her sister's idea. Going to the Train Wreck? In one way, it sounded way cool. And it would definitely be better than spending a weekend night with their mom!

But on the other hand, did they really want to barge in on a party where they didn't know ninety-nine percent of the people? And what about Alex? Riley usually spent Saturday night with her guy.

"You're forgetting one small thing," Riley said. "We haven't been invited to this party yet."

"Small detail," Chloe said. "Give me those."

She held out her hand, and Riley passed the stack of flyers to her sister.

"What are you going to do?" Riley asked.

"Give them back to Andrea, of course," Chloe said. "And when I do, I'll talk her into getting us invited to the party."

10

"Us? But I'm supposed to go out with Alex on Saturday night!" Riley protested.

"You can't! You've got to come to this party with me," Chloe insisted. "Besides, you see Alex *every* Saturday. Don't you get it? That's a problem."

"How?" Riley asked.

"You and Alex are in a rut!" Chloe declared.

No way, Riley started to say. That's not a rut. That's called going out! That's called having a social life!

But before she could open her mouth, someone tapped her on the shoulder.

Riley whirled around. Sierra Pomeroy was standing behind her. She had just breezed into California Dream. Her wavy red hair was flying wildly, draping over her black tank top. It looked amazing with her hip-hugger orange corduroy bell-bottoms and spiky boots.

"Fab news!" Sierra declared, throwing her arms open wide to make an announcement. "Guess who just got invited to play a live gig on the air at KMAL?"

"You?" Riley guessed.

"Yes!" Sierra said, practically jumping up and down in excitement.

That was easy, Riley thought. After all, The Wave was getting to be more and more popular all the time. They had played at Riley and Chloe's party a few months ago. And they got booked to play at California Dream a bunch of times, too.

11

"Awesome!" Riley said.

"Hey, that's great," Chloe congratulated her. "KMAL is a college radio station, isn't it?"

"Right," Sierra said, nodding. "Only I have a major problem, and you two have *got* to help me solve it."

"What's up?" Riley asked.

Sierra dragged Riley and Chloe over to a table where she dumped her things. She made them sit down.

"It's my mom," Sierra explained. "She will never in a million years let me play this radio station thing on Saturday."

"Well, duh," Chloe said. "She doesn't even know you're in a rock band, so how *could* she let you go?"

Sierra automatically glanced over her shoulder, as if she wanted to make sure her mom wasn't walking in the door right then.

Wow, Riley thought. It's hard leading a double life! She always has to be so careful!

Sierra's real name was Sarah, and that's what her parents and teachers called her. At home, Sarah wore really conservative clothes – the kind her mother liked – and played the violin.

But at school and around her friends, she changed her hair, changed her clothes, went by a totally different name and played bass guitar in a really cool band.

She's practically the coolest person at West Malibu High, Riley thought. Except her parents don't know it.

"See, here's the problem," Sierra explained.

"There's this big violin competition on Saturday afternoon. My mom has been insisting for months that I'm going to win it."

"Well, she's probably right," Chloe said. "You're awesome on violin."

Sierra shrugged. "I know. But I'm just so tired of having to win every single competition that comes along, you know?"

Riley nodded.

"But my mom is so worried about me getting into a good college. She wants me to have all these extracurricular talents and stuff, so they'll look good on my college applications."

"But college is four years away," Chloe said. "We just started high school."

"Tell me about it," Sierra replied.

Wow, Riley thought. No wonder she leads a double life. Her parents are so high pressure.

"Anyway, I *can't* go to the competition. Not and do the performance at KMAL," Sierra said. "Because they're both at two o'clock on Saturday afternoon. Don't you see? I've *got* to do something to get out of that violin thing – *somehow*."

Hmm, Riley thought. This was going to be hard. Unless...

"I know!" Riley's eyes lit up. "Just tell your mom you have to work on something for school. Like a science fair project or something. That would look good on your college applications."

[Riley: Okay, okay, I know what you're thinking. Nobody does the science fair in high school, except for the die-hard science geeks. Right? I know that... and you know that... but Sierra's parents don't know that. I'm willing to bet they don't have a clue! Get it?]

Sierra nodded slowly, thinking about it. Her eyes started to twinkle. "Okay, yeah. That might work. So listen – you guys have to help me. Okay?"

"No problem," Chloe and Riley both agreed. "What do we do?"

"Just cover for me," Sierra said. "I'll tell my mom I'm at your house for the next few nights, working on the science fair project."

"But you'll really be at Alex's house or Saul's, rehearsing with the band, right?" Chloe said.

Saul was the drummer in Sierra's band.

"Exactly," Sierra said.

"And what about Saturday?" Riley asked.

"Same thing," Sierra said. "I'll tell my mom we have to work on the science fair thing *all day*. But instead, we'll all be at KMAL! You guys can come, too. You'll be my groupies."

Riley laughed. "Ooh, can I have your autograph?"

"You asked for it!" Sierra said in a joking-but-you'll-be-sorry way.

Quickly, she pulled out a navy blue gel pen from her pocket and grabbed Riley's wrist. She held it tightly as she wrote "Sierra" really big on the back of Riley's hand.

14

"Gee, thanks," Riley joked. "I won't wash for a week."

The waitress zoomed over to their table on her rounds. "You girls eating again?" she asked. "Another latte? Lemonade? Bagel?"

Riley glanced at her sister.

"No," Chloe said, pushing back her chair. "We're out of here."

"Okay," Sierra said. "Just be sure to remember: if my mom calls your house for the next few days, I'm there. Right?"

"We've got your back," Riley said.

"Thanks! This is going to be so cool!" Sierra called after them.

At least Sierra's life will never be in a rut! Riley thought as they hurried home from California Dream.

Their house on the beach was just a short walk away. A few minutes later, they bounced in through the front door.

"Hello, my two beautiful ladies!" Manuelo greeted them.

Manuelo was the live-in housekeeper and cook. He was always in the kitchen, whipping up something wonderful for dinner or baking muffins for breakfast. Plus, he loved to give out advice – whether Riley and Chloe asked for it or not.

Half the time it was really helpful. The other half of the time...

"Hey, Manuelo," Riley said, sniffing the air and

15

trying to guess what was for dinner. "What are you making?"

"Baby pizzas with zucchini and cheese," he said. "But you can't have them. They're for the neighbourhood Save the Beach fundraiser."

"I hate it when you make yummy stuff for everyone else and we can't eat it," Chloe said.

"Why?" Manuelo asked, cooing in his warm, sing-song voice. "You two are never hungry after school. You just had a bagel, decaf latte and lemonade spritzer at California Dream, no?"

"No!" Chloe declared. "I didn't *touch* that bagel! And how would you know what we ordered, anyway?"

Manuelo tilted his head. "Oh, come on. I know you two like the back of my head," he said.

"Hand," Riley corrected him.

"Whatever," Manuelo said with a shrug. "So what's new with you, anyway?"

New? Riley thought. She glanced at Chloe.

Ohhhhhh, not much! We're just trying to get ourselves invited to a cool party with a bunch of seniors in a warehouse somewhere. Probably without chaperones. And we're plotting ways to fool Sierra's mom into thinking Sierra is a science nerd. And then we're going to help her sneak out of the house on Saturday so she can play in a rock band that her parents don't even know exists!

But Riley couldn't tell him any of that, could she?

"New?" Riley said. "Nothing. Nothing at all."

16

"We're just bored," Chloe said.

"Bored?" Manuelo raised an eyebrow.

"Yes," Chloe said. "Our lives are in a total rut. We need a change, Manuelo. Some way to spice things up."

Manuelo clapped his hands together. "I know!" he said brightly. "You want spice in your life? How about a new cinnamon toothpaste? We got a free sample in the mail."

Toothpaste? Was he kidding? Riley wondered.

"No thanks, Manuelo," she said. "Somehow I don't think a new toothpaste is really going to float my boat."

"Well, how about we hold dinner till eight tonight for a change?" he said. "That way, I can catch that hot new game-show host on the Spanish TV channel."

Eating late is supposed to spice up our lives? Riley thought. Poor Manuelo. He just didn't get it.

"No thanks," Chloe said. "I haven't eaten since the mystery meat at lunch. I'm starved."

"Okay, okay," Manuelo said. "We'll eat on time."

"Good." Riley grabbed an apple and headed towards the deck.

Manuelo jumped in front of her.

"I wouldn't go out there if I were you," he said. "Not if you want to get out of your rut."

"Why not?" Riley asked.

"Because what's waiting for you out there isn't going to be much of a surprise," Manuelo said.

What's waiting out there? Riley wondered. Then it hit her. Oh, no. She and Chloe exchanged glances.

This could mean only one thing: Larry was here.

Talk about predictable! Riley thought.

Larry Slotnick, the guy who lived next door, was the most predictable thing on the planet. Mainly because he was totally and completely in love with Riley. He showed up at the Carlsons' house about five times a day. At school, he followed her around like a puppy dog.

"He's here already?" Riley asked.

Manuelo nodded. "I felt sorry for him, so I gave him a baby pizza," he added, sounding apologetic and guilty.

"Manuelo!" Riley cried. "You know you're not supposed to feed him! Now he'll never go away!"

But Riley didn't really mind that much. She was used to Larry by now. He was nice enough. In fact, sometimes he was really sweet, although he was definitely *not* boyfriend material.

"Larry, what are you doing here?" Riley asked, sliding open the glass door to the deck.

"Riley, my one, my only," Larry said, clutching her hand dramatically. "I came over to warn you: the tides are going to be dangerously strong tonight. Whatever you do, *don't* go in the ocean."

Riley eyed him suspiciously. "I had no intention of going swimming at night," she said. "Everyone knows that's dangerous. What are you *really* doing here?"

Larry shrugged and let a goofy grin spread across his face. "I just wanted to see you," he admitted. "Do you want to go out with me this weekend?"

How many times a week was he going to ask her out? Riley wondered. And besides, didn't he notice that she already *had* a boyfriend?

It was almost getting to be a joke. Larry *knew* what the answer was, but she still had to tell him no. Every time.

"No thanks," Riley said. "I'm going to be busy this weekend if Chloe has anything to say about it."

"Chloe? What's she up to now?" Larry asked.

"She's trying to get us invited to the Train Wreck," Riley said. "It's this big party in a warehouse somewhere."

Oops! Maybe I shouldn't have told him, Riley thought. Now he's going to want to come along, too.

"Wow," Larry said. "Yeah, I've heard about that from my cousin. It's pretty wild, according to him."

Chloe joined them on the deck. "What's pretty wild?" she asked.

"The Train Wreck, according to Larry's cousin," Riley answered.

"That party is totally out of control," Larry said. "My cousin told me to stay away from it."

"Excellent!" Chloe said, looking totally pleased. "That's exactly what we need to spice up our lives!"

Riley giggled. It *did* sound fun to do something different. Something a little wild. Maybe even over the top.

"You'll never get invited," Larry said. "It's a seniors-only thing."

"Wrong," Chloe argued. "Andrea Ripner is going, and she's a freshman."

"She's an exception," Larry claimed. "I'm telling you – you guys will never get in."

Riley saw the look of determination flash into her sister's eyes.

Uh-oh. Riley knew that look. It was the look that said: Don't even *think* about trying to stop Chloe Carlson when she puts her mind to something!

"You want to bet?" Chloe said, putting her hands on her hips.

Oh, boy. Here we go! Riley thought.

"Definitely," Larry said. He held out his hand to shake on it. "What do I get if I win? A date with Riley?"

"No way!" Riley blurted out.

"I'll make you a batch of my famous blond brownies," Chloe offered. Riley glanced at her. "Okay, Riley will help me, since I'm not exactly the world's best cook. Plus you'll have the satisfaction of knowing you've beaten me, which would be enough of a reward – except it isn't going to happen."

"Okay, you're on," Larry said.

They shook on it, and Riley saw her sister's eyes dancing.

"I swear I'm going to get us into that party – if it's the last thing I do!" Chloe declared.

chapter
three

"Here she comes," Amanda Grey whispered to Chloe the next day at lunch. Amanda was one of Chloe's good friends at West Malibu High. Chloe had just finished explaining about how she was in a rut and needed Andrea Ripner to get her invited to the Train Wreck.

> [Chloe: Don't look at me like that – as if I'm
> being a bad friend by not inviting Amanda to
> come to the Train Wreck, too. The truth is, she
> would never in a million years come even if I
> did ask her. What? You don't believe me? Okay,
> then watch this.]

"Listen, Amanda, do you want me to try to get you invited, too?" Chloe asked.

"I can't. My mom would never let me go," Amanda said, shaking her head really fast. "No thanks, but thanks anyway, Chloe."

[Chloe: See? What did I tell you?]

"You'd better hurry if you want to catch her," Amanda urged, nodding towards Andrea Ripner.

"Is she alone?" Chloe asked. She didn't want to just turn around and look.

"Yes," Amanda said. "She's trying to find a seat."

Okay, Chloe thought. Perfect. She grabbed the stack of party flyers from her backpack, stood up and walked towards Andrea. "Oh, hi!" she said. "I was just coming to look for you."

"Me?" Andrea said, sort of surprised.

"Yeah," Chloe answered. "I wanted to give you these." She held out the flyers. "You left them at California Dream yesterday."

Andrea glanced at the papers in Chloe's hand. "Can you set them on my tray?" She nodded her head towards the crowded surface.

"Sure, but...maybe you should wait till you put your tray down. Do you want to eat with us?" Chloe asked. "We're sitting right over there."

Andrea glanced around, trying to find her own friends. But it was still early. She didn't spot anyone she knew. "Okay," she said with a shrug. "Whatever."

Excellent! Chloe thought. This was going exactly as she had planned!

The two of them sat down, and Chloe handed the flyers over. Then she introduced Andrea to Amanda.

"Hi," Amanda said softly.

"So tell me about this party!" Chloe plunged right

22

into the conversation. "It sounds totally awesome!"

"It is," Andrea said, clearly glowing with pride that she was in with a senior crowd. "Unbelievable bands."

Wow, Chloe thought. "So do you think you could get me and my sister invited?" she asked.

Andrea took a bite of her chicken salad and shook her head. "It's a seniors party," she said with her mouth still full.

"I know." Chloe leaned forward. "But Riley and I are *so* ready to be hanging out with an older crowd. I mean, don't you just find the freshman parties totally dull?"

Chloe could feel Amanda giving her a strange look. As if she thought Chloe was being phony. Pretending to be too cool for freshmen or something.

Okay, maybe I am overdoing it a bit, Chloe thought.

She sat back a little. "I mean, Riley and I are kind of in a social rut," Chloe said honestly. "Going to the Train Wreck would be such a great way to get out of it."

Andrea laughed. "Yeah, but it's not going to happen," she said. "I'm really sorry, but I'm, like, the only freshman invited. Not even many juniors get to go."

"So how come you're so lucky?" Amanda asked.

"Because I'm friends with Dan, and he runs it," Andrea explained. "He pays for everything – the food, the drinks, the bands – and then everyone gives him five dollars at the door. So he gets to make the rules. And he says no freshmen."

"Except for you." Chloe repeated the obvious.

Andrea smiled and shrugged. "What can I say?"

"Isn't there any chance you could talk him into making one more exception?" Chloe said. "I mean, Riley and I would just hang out and be cool. And we'd pay the five dollars, and we wouldn't eat or drink a thing…"

Andrea shook her head and took a gulp of her grape soda.

"Well, how about if you just tell us where the party is?" Chloe pleaded. "Riley and I could show up, and Dan would never have to know you're the one who gave us the address."

Andrea shook her head again and started to say, "Sorry."

But she was in the middle of taking another sip. Grape soda dribbled out of her mouth. It dripped down the front of her pink sweater.

"Oh, man!" she said, grabbing some napkins and blotting at the mess furiously.

"Here." Chloe quickly offered her some more napkins.

But the stain had already soaked in.

"Club soda would help," Amanda suggested quietly.

"Yeah, but they don't sell it in the drinks machine," Andrea moaned. She stood up, staring at the stain in horror. "What am I going to do now? I'm supposed to have my picture taken for the freshman yearbook today during fifth period!"

"How awful!" Chloe said. She knew how important it was to look good in the yearbook. She and Riley had already had their pictures taken, last week.

This is a disaster, Chloe thought. She could see in a heartbeat that the sweater Andrea was wearing matched her outfit perfectly.

"Why don't you go home during lunch and change?" Amanda suggested.

"How? I don't drive, and anyway, I live too far away," Andrea said.

Oh, gosh, Chloe thought. Wasn't there some way she could help? "I have an idea!" she blurted out. "I have a sweater almost exactly like that."

"So?" Andrea was still frowning and dabbing at the stain.

"So come home to my house right now," Chloe urged her. "I live close by. You can change into my sweater and wear it for the picture later today."

"Really?" Andrea looked up, her eyes grateful.

"Definitely," Chloe said.

"Okay, thanks!" she said as she gathered up her things and dumped the rest of her food in the trash.

You're welcome! Chloe thought. And if you want to thank me some more, maybe you'll give in and tell me the address for the Train Wreck!

Chloe quickly dumped her lunch, too, and led the way to the back door of the school. By cutting across the parking lot, they could take the shortest route to her house.

On the way, she quizzed Andrea, trying to find out how she got to be friends with Dan. But Andrea didn't say much.

"Oh, he just hangs around with some people I know." Duh, Chloe thought. W*ho*?

"People my brother knows," Andrea finally said.

So that was it! Chloe seemed to remember that Andrea had an older brother. He was at least five years older, maybe six. He had graduated already.

"Is it cool having an older brother?" Chloe asked.

"Sometimes," Andrea said. "Except when he's making you look like a jerk in front of his friends."

Hmm. That didn't sound ideal. On the other hand, Dan didn't seem to think Andrea was a jerk, did he?

"Here we are," Chloe announced, pointing to her home – a big, modern white house with lots of windows, facing the ocean. "You want the tour?"

"Not right now. Let's just hurry," Andrea said. "I don't want to be late getting back."

Okay, Chloe thought. She opened the front door. "Manuelo? Mom? I'm home!" Chloe called.

"Upstairs," Manuelo's voice answered.

"Come on," Chloe said, leading the way. She raced up the steps, turned the corner into her room, and gasped. "Manuelo! What are you doing?" she cried.

Her room was a total and complete mess! All the clothes from her closet were piled up on the bed. The dresser drawers were open and empty. The contents were strewn all over the place. Manuelo had stacked her

26

and Riley's things on her desk, the floor and the chairs.

"Oh, hi," Manuelo said, turning around and grinning. "Surprise!"

"What are you doing?" Chloe repeated, her voice rising in a panic.

"I'm trying to get you out of your rut!" Manuelo announced cheerfully. "I thought it would be a fun change for you. I'm putting Riley's things in your side of the closet and your things in her side. See? It's a whole new wardrobe... or a new way to look at things... or something."

Chloe closed her eyes, not wanting to see the mess. She knew Manuelo meant well, but this wasn't the kind of change she needed. Not at all.

And especially not right now!

"Manuelo! Did you see my pink boat-neck sweater?" she asked him desperately. "Andrea needs to borrow it."

"Pink?" he said, gazing around at the piles of clothes everywhere. "Umm..."

"Never mind," Chloe said. "Just let me look for it. Okay?"

"Sorry," Manuelo said as he tiptoed out of the room. "I thought you'd like the change."

"Oh, man," Andrea moaned, staring at the piles of clothes. "Don't tell me we skipped lunch for nothing!"

"No, no, don't worry," Chloe said. "It's here. Somewhere. It's got to be."

Chloe started digging through the clothes on the

bed. She didn't want to just dump everything on the floor, so she kept handing things to Andrea. But Andrea couldn't hold that much, so she kept putting armloads of jeans and skirts and tops back on the bed.

It was a mess.

Finally Chloe found it. At the bottom. But it was way too wrinkled. It looked awful. Chloe would never wear it like that, not even if someone paid her.

"Well, here it is," she said, holding the sweater up with a weak smile.

"You've got to be kidding me," Andrea said. "Even this stain looks better than that thing."

That was true, Chloe thought. The stain was better.

"I'm really sorry," she said. "I mean, maybe we can iron it or something. Do you want me to try?"

"No thanks," Andrea said, turning to leave. She glanced at her watch and sighed. "Great. Now we're going to be late for class, too. What a waste of time."

"Sorry," Chloe called, running to catch up with her. "Hey, wait – do you want to borrow something else?"

But Andrea was already on her way out of the front door.

Whoa, Chloe thought, hearing the door slam. That didn't work out – *at all*. And now we'll never get invited to the party, she thought. For sure.

chapter
four

"**S**o don't forget," Sierra said to Riley after school that day. "I'm at your house, right? We're working on the science fair project."

"Got it," Riley said. "Don't worry! Go."

"Thanks." Sierra gave her a big smile and started to dash off down the crowded hallway.

"Wait!" Riley called.

Sierra's red hair fluttered as she spun around. "What?"

"Come back!" Riley said, motioning.

The bell had just rung after last period, so the halls were full. Sierra weaved her way back through the crowd.

Riley fished around in her backpack for a small note, folded in half twice, written in lime-green gel pen on black paper. Finally she found it. "Give this to Alex," she said, handing the note to Sierra.

Sierra sighed. "Not another one. Okay, but I'm reading it," she said.

Hey! Riley thought. That's personal!

But there was no point in trying to stop Sierra. She was like that. And besides, Sierra already knew what it said.

It was exactly like the five other notes Riley had given Alex last week. And exactly like the six notes Alex had given her. It just said "hi".

"You guys have been doing this for a week now," Sierra said. "Isn't it getting a little stale?"

"Not to me." Riley smiled inside and out.

[**Riley**: **Don't say it, because I've already heard it a dozen times from Chloe. Rut, rut, rut. So maybe she's right, but I'll never be tired of getting little pieces of paper from Alex with "hi" written on them. So what if it seems dumb to everyone else? This is one rut that I happen to like!**]

Sierra stuffed the note in her pocket and rolled her eyes. "Hopeless romantics," she said. She whirled around and sped off to her band rehearsal.

Riley closed her locker and hurried to meet Chloe at their usual spot. For some reason, she hadn't seen her sister all day and she was eager to find out what had happened with Andrea.

"Well, did you do it?" she asked, cutting straight to the chase. "Did you get us invited to the Train Wreck?"

"No," Chloe said with a shudder. "It was a disaster."

She filled Riley in on all the details of the lunch meeting with Andrea. The spilled grape soda. The sweater fiasco.

"Oops," Riley said.

"Yeah," Chloe agreed, heading towards the school's parking lot. "Anyway, I want to find out how the picture went. Andrea usually hangs around outside after school. I'm going to try to talk to her."

"But isn't she usually with Dan and his friends?" Riley asked.

Chloe nodded.

"Wow. I mean, you're just going to walk up to a bunch of seniors and start talking?" Riley asked.

Chloe swallowed hard and nodded. Riley could see that she was nervous already.

"I *should* be able to talk to them," Chloe argued. "How are we supposed to fit in at this party if we can't even talk to them?"

"We're *not*," Riley told her. "That's why we're not invited."

"You can wait here if you want," Chloe said, "but I'm going up to them. Andrea's just a freshman, anyway."

Riley stayed back a little, hovering just behind her sister. Not enough to seem as if she was avoiding the older group. Just enough to stay clear of the dagger looks that some of the senior girls were shooting in their direction.

"Hi," Chloe said to Andrea.

"Hi," Andrea said, just barely glancing at Chloe.

Whoa, Riley thought, watching her sister. Chloe was being totally bold. Riley was impressed.

Dan and his friends all leaned on someone's Range Rover, talking about something they'd seen on MTV. They didn't stop their conversation when Chloe approached.

"Listen, I'm sorry about the sweater," Chloe said softly to Andrea.

"No biggie," Andrea said with a shrug.

"So how did it go in fifth period?" Chloe asked.

"What?" Andrea looked clueless.

"The yearbook picture," Chloe explained.

"Oh. Fine," Andrea said. "The photographer said he's coming back tomorrow, so I didn't have to do it today."

"Great!" Chloe's voice was a little too loud.

Dan and one of his friends stopped talking. Their heads snapped in her direction.

"What's so great?" the other guy asked.

"Nothing," Andrea answered quickly, not letting Chloe talk. "Really. So what happened on TRL?" she asked Dan. She turned her back just a little, so Chloe and Riley were shut out of the group.

Ouch! Riley thought. Talk about being ignored!

But Chloe held her head up high and tossed her hair over her shoulders.

"Come on," she said to Riley. "We've got stuff to do at home."

"Stuff? Like what?" Riley asked.

"Just wait. You'll find out," Chloe said in a grim voice.

A few minutes later, when they climbed the stairs to their room, Riley saw what her sister was talking about. Their room was a mess! Manuelo hadn't touched a thing since lunch.

"This is his idea of putting some spice in our lives?" Riley moaned.

"He meant well," Chloe explained, staring helplessly at the piles and piles of clothes. "He thought it would give us a change."

"Yeah. Sort of like having all your hair chopped off by a team of wild monkeys would be a change," Riley said. "Not exactly what we had in mind."

"I know," Chloe agreed. "So what do we do? You want my side of the closet?"

"No thanks. I liked my side fine. I'm used to it. I know where everything is. At least, I *used* to know."

Chloe nodded and started putting her sweaters back in her dresser drawers. Riley pitched in, too. She picked up a little brown skirt from the top of the pile.

"Hey," she said. "I forgot I had this. And it's so cute! It goes with my pink-and-brown-and-white-striped top."

"See?" Chloe said. "Maybe Manuelo *did* do us a favour."

"Someone did you a favour?" a voice asked from the doorway.

Riley turned and saw her mother, Macy Carlson, standing there with a big smile.

"Hi, guys," Macy said. "Who did you a favour?"

33

"Oh, nobody," Riley explained, not wanting to go into the whole thing.

Then she saw the look on her mom's face – the one that said: How come you never tell me anything any more? My girls are growing up so fast.

Poor Mom! Riley thought. She can't stand it that we're not little kids any more!

"I was talking about Manuelo," Riley explained. "He's trying to help us get out of our rut."

"Oh, right!" Macy said. "He told me about that. That's why I came up to talk to you."

Uh-oh, Riley thought. What now?

"Well, I have a great idea to get you out of your slump!" Macy added. "You know how we always do the same thing every Friday night? And it's getting to be such an old, boring routine?"

"Tell me about it," Chloe said.

"So here's my idea," Macy said, excited. "How about if we go out on *Saturday* instead of Friday?"

"That's it?" Riley asked, amazed.

She stared at her mother, openmouthed. Her mom was usually pretty cool – for a mom. She was a fashion designer, for one thing. And she liked a lot of trendy music. And she got along really well with their dad, even though they were separated. And she never ever lectured Chloe and Riley about stupid things like watching too much TV. But even so, Riley couldn't help wondering: Could parents possibly be more dense?

"That's your plan to spice up our lives?" Riley asked. "Go out on Saturday instead of Friday?"

"Yes." Macy nodded. "And instead of going to the Siam Palace, we try that new place across the street. It's opening on Saturday – and kids eat free!"

Kids eat free. Just the phrase we want to hear when we're trying to get ourselves invited to a cool, senior party, Riley thought.

She glanced at Chloe and saw the look of panic on her face. She knew what Chloe was thinking: Saturday was the night of the party!

They couldn't go out with their mom that night – not if they were going to the Train Wreck! Not if Chloe wanted to win her bet with Larry!

"Uh, that sounds good, Mom," Riley said, trying to think of some excuse. "But, uh, the thing is, even though we're in a rut, we kind of like to stick with the traditions."

"Traditions?" Macy said. "Oh, come on, Riley. Traditions are for remote rainforest tribes, where they don't have malls or anything."

Riley did a double take. "That's what Chloe said!" she cried. "What are you two – related or something?"

Macy laughed. "Seriously, wouldn't you like a change?" she asked.

Sure, Riley thought. We'd like to spend *both* weekend nights doing something *fun*. Like going to this party.

Before she could think of a good excuse for dumping her mom's plan, the phone rang.

Both girls could hear it – the cordless phone was buried somewhere under the piles of clothes on their bed. They started tossing sweaters and jeans aside, trying to unearth the handset.

Chloe found it first. "Hello?" she said.

Riley waited.

"No, sorry, wrong number. No one here named Sarah," she said and hung up.

Sarah? Riley's eyes flashed wide in alarm. Oh, no! she thought. That must have been Sierra's mom!

How could Chloe do that? We were supposed to be covering for her! Riley tried to signal Chloe that she'd just made a huge mistake, but Chloe didn't seem to get it.

"Uh, listen, Mom," Riley said, chattering fast. "Can we talk about this later? We've got to do our homework."

"Homework? Oh, sure, okay," Macy agreed happily. "Whatever. We'll work it out."

Riley waited till her mom was out of the door and down the stairs before yelling at Chloe.

"That was Sierra's mom!" she said. "And you told her…"

The phone rang again. Riley dived for it. "Hello?" she said, hoping it was Mrs. Pomeroy again.

"Um… hello? I'm trying to reach my daughter, Sarah," the voice said. "Is she there?"

"Yes!" Riley said eagerly. "She's here! Hi!"

I sound like an idiot, Riley thought. But she didn't

care. She just wanted to cover for Sierra.

"May I speak to her?" Mrs. Pomeroy asked.

"Uh, you could..." Riley tried to think fast. "But, uh, she's in the bathroom right now. And when you called a minute ago, my sister had just walked in, so she didn't know Sarah was here."

"Oh. Okay," Mrs. Pomeroy said, sounding as though she bought about ninety-nine percent of that. "Well, could you have her call me right back?"

Call you right back? Uh, sure, Riley thought. I guess so. Somehow.

"Definitely," Riley said, trying to sound as if everything were fine.

"Thanks," Mrs. Pomeroy said before hanging up.

As soon as she had a dial tone, Riley started punching numbers again.

"What's wrong?" Chloe asked.

"Sierra's mom," Riley explained. "She wants to talk to Sierra. I'm calling her mobile."

"I wonder why her mom didn't do that," Chloe said.

Good question, Riley thought.

Her heart pounded nervously, waiting for the call to go through.

Come on, Sierra, she thought as the phone rang. Pick up. Pick up.

"No answer?" Chloe asked.

Riley shook her head.

"She probably can't hear it ringing because the band is practising," Chloe said.

Of course! Riley thought.

"I'll bet her mom called her mobile first and didn't get an answer," Riley said. "And now she's waiting for Sierra to call her back. What are we going to do?"

Chloe bit her finger. "I don't know. But we'd better think of something. We *promised* Sierra we'd cover for her!"

"Okay," Riley said. She started dialling the phone again.

"What are you doing?" Chloe asked.

"Following my rule number one: When in doubt, stall for time."

As soon as Sierra's mom answered, Riley said, "Hello, Mrs. Pomeroy? This is Riley. Um, Sarah is still in the bathroom, so she asked me to call you and take a message."

"Fine," her mother said. "Just tell her that we've had a change of plans. I'm going to have to pick her up at your house early."

Early?

"Uh, when?" Riley asked.

"In about twenty minutes," Mrs. Pomeroy said before hanging up.

"Oh, no!" Riley cried.

"What?" Chloe asked, clearly worried.

"She's coming in twenty minutes!" Riley explained. "We've got to run over to Alex's house, where the band is rehearsing, and get Sierra – right now!"

chapter
five

It's a good thing it almost never rains in Malibu, Riley thought as she ran the mile to Alex's house, where the band was rehearsing. Because if it *had* been raining, she'd have to walk in and face Alex with her hair hanging in straggly wet clumps.

It's bad enough that I'm all sweaty and out of breath, Riley thought. And I didn't even have time to fix my lip gloss.

But who cared? This was an emergency!

She dashed down the basement steps and waved her arms wildly at the band, trying to get them to stop. They were in the middle of a really loud number.

Sierra nodded and smiled and kept playing. As if she thought Riley was just waving a really big, happy hello. Or acting like a groupie in the audience or something.

"Sierra!" Riley screamed, trying to be heard. "Your mom called!"

Sierra made a face. "What?"

Frantically, Riley made the sign for "cut", gesturing with a hand motion across her neck.

"We've got to go!" she shouted.

Saul, the drummer, finally got the message and stopped playing. Then the other musicians stopped, too.

"Hi," Alex said, grinning at Riley. Clearly he was happy to see her. "I got your note."

"Hi," she said, grinning back.

For a second, she was stuck in a grin-fest, just smiling at him like an idiot and thinking about how cute he looked with his baby blue T-shirt and sandy-blond hair.

"What's up?" Sierra asked, snapping her out of it.

"Your mom called," Riley said. "She's on her way to my house to pick you up. Like, right now!"

"Uh-oh. Sorry, guys," Sierra said, throwing her bass guitar in its case. "Gotta go."

She hoisted her backpack with her books and a change of clothes in it but left her guitar in Alex's basement so her mom wouldn't see it.

"I almost blew your cover," Riley confessed as they hurried back towards her house.

"You *can't*," Sierra said. "You've got to make this work for me! We are so psyched about playing at the radio station on Saturday."

"I know, I know. I'm sorry," Riley said. "But don't worry – it's okay. I think I fixed it."

"How?" Sierra asked.

"I told your mom you were in the bathroom," Riley said. "And—"

She stopped in midsentence. A car had just passed them as they walked along the road. It looked a whole lot like Sierra's mom's dark green minivan.

Riley's throat felt tight. "Was that your mom?"

Sierra sort of ducked and turned her face away. "Yeah. Did she see us?"

The car slowed down. Stopped. Then started backing up.

"Yup," Riley said. "She's coming back."

"Oh, no!" Sierra moaned. "Look at me!"

Riley glanced over and realised what the problem was. Sierra was wearing a tiny little T-shirt with the name of some alternative band on it. It was so short that with her tight low-slung jeans, her navel showed.

The pink leather slides with high platform heels didn't help either. She had changed into these clothes that morning after she got to school.

"She's going to kill me!" Sierra muttered between clenched teeth.

Her mother pulled up beside them and rolled the passenger-side window down. "Sarah?" she said, her voice cold and shocked. "What on *earth* are you wearing, young lady?"

"Mom…" Sierra started to say in a don't-get-on-my-case voice.

She shot a glance at Riley. Her eyes said, Help!

Riley's heart pounded. Think, she told herself. Quick!

41

All at once, it came to her.

"Oh, those are my clothes, Mrs. Pomeroy," Riley explained. "I, uh, spilled grape soda all over Sarah while we were working on the science fair project. So I loaned her an outfit of mine."

"Oh." Mrs. Pomeroy nodded. "I see." She stared at her daughter again, looking at her feet. "You even spilled on her shoes?" she asked.

"Um, no, no," Riley said quickly. "But I talked her into trying my shoes on, since she had to change the rest of her outfit."

"Oh." Her mother didn't look too happy about that. "Well, what are you doing outside? Are you finished with the project?"

"No," Sierra answered fast. "We just had to get some air. You know, to clear our heads... after all that science."

"Right!" Riley agreed. "The science was so... so heavy."

Mrs. Pomeroy looked like she was trying to believe them but that it was hard. Riley could tell she was thinking about it. After all, it hadn't been very long since she had called and Riley had claimed Sierra was in the bathroom.

When did Riley have time to spill all that grape soda all over Sierra, and then change, and then go for a walk?

"Get in," her mother said, frowning. "We're in a hurry. Your dad and I are going out tonight."

42

Sierra climbed in the car with a scowl on her face. Neither of the Pomeroys looked too happy.

"Talk to you later," Riley called as they pulled away.

Sierra didn't even nod or answer.

"You look so glum, like a glum little pineapple," Manuelo said, clearly trying to tease Riley out of her bad mood at dinner that night.

"You haven't even touched your food," her mother said.

Riley poked at her chicken and forced herself to smile. "It's nothing," she said. "I'm just, you know…" Her voice trailed off. She couldn't tell them what was really bothering her.

It's not really my fault that Sierra's mom came driving along and saw Sierra in those clothes, Riley tried to tell herself. But still, she felt awful. She had promised to cover for her friend, and somehow she felt as though she'd let Sierra down.

"You're just in a rut," Manuelo declared. As if that were the whole problem in a nutshell. "And I know what always cheers my little pineapples up when they're unhappy."

"What?" Chloe asked.

Yeah, what? Riley thought. She held her breath. Not more rearranging clothes, she hoped.

"Shopping!" Manuelo announced with a big smile.

"Seriously?" Riley's face lit up.

"Totally!" Chloe agreed, perking up, too.

43

[Riley: Honestly, just the mention of the word "shopping" can cheer Chloe and me up. And you know what? It isn't even about buying stuff. It's just the fun of wandering through the stores and thinking about what we might want to get. I remember once when we were ten, my dad gave us twenty dollars to spend on anything we wanted – just out of the blue, for no reason at all! It was an amazing feeling. We went shopping five times before we even spent a dime! Manuelo really knows how to cheer a girl up, you know?]

Riley took a bite of Manuelo's famous chicken diablo. It was delicious.

"Well, since I am so sorry about messing up your room and your clothes today, I thought I should come up with a better idea," Manuelo explained. "My suggestion is this: Why don't you go shopping tomorrow after school? You can each buy a new outfit."

"Really?" Riley's eyes brightened, and she glanced at her mom.

Macy nodded. "Manuelo told me about it earlier, and I agree," she said. "I'll even let you use my credit card."

"Cool!" Chloe bubbled with excitement. "We could definitely use some new clothes," she added.

Chloe shot a glance at Riley, and Riley knew instantly what her sister was thinking.

The party on Saturday night.

They needed new outfits to wear.

Yeah, Riley thought. They needed something cool and hip and… and… *older*-looking for the Train Wreck.

"Thanks!" Riley said, jumping up to give Manuelo and her mom a hug.

As soon as dinner was over, she dashed upstairs and called Sierra. "How's it going?" she asked Sierra in a low voice.

"Okay," Sierra reported. "But it took a lot of explaining. My mom wanted to see the soda stains. I had to tell her I left my clothes at your house. Tomorrow I'm going to have to pour grape soda on that white crewneck sweater. Boo-hoo."

Riley laughed. She knew the white sweater was Sierra's *least* favourite piece of clothing in the whole world. But her mom loved it.

"Good," Riley said. "I'll even buy the grape soda. And you can pretend to pick up your clothes when you come over tomorrow to work on the science fair. Only guess what we'll be doing instead?"

"What?" Sierra asked.

"Shopping!" Riley cheered. "Can you come with us?"

"For sure," Sierra said. "Saul can't practise tomorrow, so we're not having a band rehearsal. But my mom said if this science fair project is so important, we should work on it every day. She's practically *forcing* me to come over your house tomorrow! Can you believe that?"

"Great!" Riley said. "We're buying new outfits to wear on Saturday. Maybe you can get something new, too. For the radio station gig."

"Awesome," Sierra said. "Okay. But listen, we can't get caught. My mom is getting so suspicious. If I mess up one more time—"

"Don't worry," Riley interrupted. "We'll figure something out. I promise – no more mistakes."

chapter six

"**E**w. What is it?" Chloe made a face and stared at the breakfast plate Manuelo had just put in front of her.

"Surprise," Manuelo said proudly. "No more breakfast rut! I made everything different and special for both of you."

"Different? How?" Riley asked.

"Tomato muffins instead of blueberry," Manuelo explained. "And Peking duck pancakes. You want juice?"

He held out a glass with something bright green in it.

"Juice?" Chloe stared at it weakly.

"Kiwi juice," Manuelo explained.

Chloe's heart sank. Oh, no, she thought. He was trying to spice up their lives again.

How long was this going to go on?

She forced herself to smile. "Gee, that's great, Manuelo," she said. She took a sip of the kiwi juice. It was so sour, her lips puckered.

"You like?" Manuelo asked. "It makes your lips look all big and pouty, like a model's."

"I'd rather have plain old OJ," Chloe muttered under her breath, but she didn't want to hurt Manuelo's feelings. She knew he was just trying to be sweet.

She ate a piece of Peking duck pancake and tried to drown out the taste with maple syrup.

Ick. Syrup and duck didn't go together too well.

A minute later, Larry appeared on the deck, waving to be let in. "Hi!" he said when Manuelo opened the door. "What's for breakfast? Mmm, tomato muffins!"

He popped one into his mouth, whole.

Typical Larry, Chloe thought. He was so weird, he *liked* tomato muffins!

"I'd kill for our boring old oatmeal and fruit," Chloe whispered to Riley.

"I know," she agreed quietly.

They picked at their food and then left when Manuelo wasn't looking. Larry tagged along, walking with them to school.

"So I'm winning our bet, aren't I?" he taunted Chloe.

"No way," Chloe said. "We're going to the Train Wreck. We just haven't been invited yet."

"Yet?" Larry repeated. "You hate to admit it, but I'm right about this. Andrea will never get you an invitation."

He sounded so sure, Chloe began to have doubts. What if he *was* right? What if, no matter how much she begged, Andrea wouldn't give in?

"Hey, I didn't say that we'd get *invited*," Chloe reminded Larry. "I just said we'd get *into* the party. That's the bet, right?"

"So what?" Larry shrugged. "You don't even know where the party is. How are you going to get in?"

Chloe's brain raced. Maybe I've been going about this all wrong, she thought. Forget Andrea.

"All we have to do is find out who Rafe is!" Chloe declared. "And ask him the usual question."

"What's the usual question?" Riley asked.

Chloe thought for a minute. "It's got to be the something obvious – like 'Where's the party?'"

Larry chuckled and shook his head. "You're going to lose," he teased Chloe.

We'll see about that, she thought.

She wasn't ready to give up yet!

As soon as she got the chance, Chloe skipped out of homeroom and headed for the library. She pulled a copy of last year's yearbook off the shelf and started turning the pages.

One of Chloe's friends, Tara Jordan, was in the library, too, working on a research paper. She scooted her chair next to Chloe's and leaned over.

"What's up?" Tara asked.

"Long story," Chloe said. "Riley and I are trying to find some guy named Rafe."

"How come?" she asked.

"Oh, it's just a stupid bet I have with Larry," Chloe

49

said. She kind of left out the senior party stuff on purpose. It would be too weird to mention a cool party that Chloe couldn't invite her friend to.

"Say no more," Tara said, rolling her eyes. "So, what's with the yearbook?"

"I think Rafe must be one of the senior guys," Chloe explained. "So I'm looking at last year's juniors."

"Clever."

She watched as Chloe turned the pages.

"Hey, what about him?" Tara pointed to a picture of five guys on the basketball team. "Look, it's 'Rage' Anderson. Are you sure the guy's name is Rafe? Maybe it's Rage."

"Rage?" Chloe thought about it. Could be.

Maybe it was a mistake on the flyer.

"I've heard about him," Tara went on. "He's supposed to have a horrible temper. I heard he got into a fight with a teacher last year, and he got suspended for two weeks."

"Seriously?" Chloe's eyes were wide.

Tara nodded. "Everyone says he flies off the handle really easily," she said. "That's why they call him Rage."

Whoa, freaky, Chloe thought. She didn't exactly want to walk up to a madman and get her head bitten off!

"I've seen him around," Tara said. "His shoulders are so huge, it looks like he's got no neck."

"Yeah," Chloe agreed. "I think he has a locker near my next class."

"So what do you have to do to win the bet?" Tara asked.

"I'll tell you if I win," Chloe said.

"Well, good luck," Tara called as Chloe gathered up her books.

Thanks, Chloe thought. I'll need it!

She wasn't sure she even wanted to *talk* to someone named Rage. But she had to do it if she wanted to go to the party and win the bet.

She hurried to get her things for her next class, then waited for the bell. Finally, the halls began to fill.

There he is, Chloe thought.

He had really short hair and he was letting the stubble on his chin grow. Plus he was at least six feet tall. He towered over Chloe.

Her heart jumped a beat as she walked up to him. "Uh, hi. You're Rage, right?" she said, trying to sound confident.

"Huh," he grunted as if he couldn't believe she was talking to him.

"Listen, someone told me to ask you: Where's the Train Wreck this weekend?" Chloe asked, staring up at him.

Rage smirked. "You've got to ask Rafe," he said. Then he smirked some more. "Like he'd tell *you*."

Chloe felt her whole face turning red. She tried to say something, but her voice wouldn't work.

"Okay, thanks." She mouthed the words, although the sound didn't come out.

How embarrassing! A bunch of people were watching her. She wanted to melt into the floor.

"Thanks," Chloe finally said, backing away and hurrying to her class.

The next two periods dragged on endlessly. It took that long for her to feel like she was anything other than a bug. A little freshman bug that guys like Rage Anderson could squash easily.

Finally she ran into Riley, between fifth and sixth periods, and told her what had happened.

"Totally embarrassing," Riley agreed. "But that's genius! You're right. Rafe is probably a senior guy. And I know who!"

"You do?" Chloe's face lit up. "That's excellent! Who?"

"Come on." Riley grabbed Chloe's hand. "He's in the art room right now."

Together the girls raced through the halls and down two flights of stairs. Chloe let Riley lead the way.

"There," Riley said, pointing to a kid working on a pastel drawing. "Him."

"Him? But that's Rafael What's-his-name," Chloe said.

"D'Antonnio," Riley said, nodding. "The exchange student from Italy. I'll bet they call him Rafe for short!"

"I bet you're right!" Chloe said. "Okay, your turn. Go ask him where the party is."

"Me?" Riley backed away. "No, no. You do it."

"I can't!" Chloe pleaded. "I'm too bummed about

what happened with Rage. You go. Please? And hurry! Before the bell rings and we're both late to class. You want to go to the Train Wreck, don't you?"

"Yeah," Riley admitted. "I was starting to get excited about it."

"So go!" Chloe urged her.

Riley took a deep breath and shook her head. "I don't know about this," she said. "Here goes nothing." She marched into the art room and put on her best smile. "Uh, hi, Rafe."

The Italian student turned and gave her a big smile. His wavy dark hair fell into his eyes and down the back of his neck.

"Hi," he said in a deep voice with a cute accent.

Chloe watched from the hall and tried not to giggle.

"Listen, I just wanted to ask you: Where's the party?" Riley said.

Rafael flashed her another flirty smile and leaned close. "It's anywhere you want it to be," he said. "How about I pick you up tonight?"

He thinks she's flirting with him! Chloe thought.

"No, um, I mean this weekend," Riley stammered. "The Train Wreck? Where is it?"

Rafael looked puzzled, but he kept grinning at her. "My house? Just you and me?" he said.

Then he winked at her. He actually winked!

No *one* winks, Chloe thought.

Riley ran out of the room, and the two of them burst into laughter.

53

"I don't believe that just happened!" Riley said as they raced to their next classes. "Now I'll have to spend the whole rest of the year avoiding him."

"Or you could go to his house this weekend," Chloe teased.

"Thanks a lot!" Riley elbowed her sister in the ribs. She covered her face with her hands. "I hope no one saw that."

"Hey, cheer up," Chloe said. "We're going shopping tonight, remember? With Mom's credit card!"

Riley sort of shrugged. "What for?" she said. "I mean, who needs a new outfit if we can't get invited to the party?"

That's true, Chloe thought.

They might have new clothes in a couple of hours, but their lives were still in a rut – with nowhere to go, nothing to do and nowhere special to wear them!

chapter
seven

"**H**ow do I look?" Riley asked, striking a pose as she held a long red sweater with a fake-fur collar up against her.

Riley, Sierra and Chloe had just wandered into a new boutique in the mall.

"You look like you're wearing a small weasel," Sierra answered. "Not good."

"A weasel?" Riley yanked the sweater away from her body and stared at it.

"Yeah," Sierra nodded. "On second thoughts, maybe you should buy it."

"Why?" Riley looked puzzled.

"So maybe Andrea will let you go to the Train Wreck, since you'll be wearing a member of her own species," Sierra joked.

"Oh, come on," Chloe said, laughing. "Andrea isn't *that* bad."

"She isn't that good," Sierra argued. "If she were

really a friend of yours, she wouldn't have snubbed you like that in the parking lot yesterday."

"You heard about that?" Chloe asked.

"I *saw* it," Sierra explained. "On my way out."

"Well, anyway, she's *not* a friend of ours," Riley pointed out. "Which is why she doesn't really *have* to invite us to the party."

"And so far she hasn't," Chloe said.

"So why are we shopping?" Sierra asked.

"Wash your mouth out!" Chloe teased. "That's not a real question!"

The three girls laughed and strolled out of the boutique. Most of the clothes in there were too expensive anyway, Riley thought.

"Where to?" Sierra asked. "We've hit every store in the mall except the department stores."

"This place is cleaned out," Riley said. "It's like they just sold everything in our sizes a few days ago."

"We could *try* a department store," Sierra said. "They're having a big sale at Birch's. I know because my mom mentioned it. And sometimes they have cute things – especially in the departments my mom *never* lets me shop in."

"Okay," Riley agreed. "Let's check it out."

Sierra led the way to the Trendsetters section on the second floor. It was filled with lots of fun things to wear – and everything was marked down.

"Wow," Riley said, racing through the racks of clothes. "You're right! This place is awesome!"

56

Within a few minutes, Sierra had found two great outfits and Chloe had found a really cute little dress.

Riley ploughed through the racks of tops that were on sale. Tons of them were adorable.

"I'll be in the dressing room," Sierra called, carrying two miniskirts in one hand and two tops, including a stretchy blue leopard print, in the other.

"Be right there," Riley answered, still going through another sale rack.

Chloe held up the dress, debating. It was a long-sleeved black sweater-dress with a hood. "What do you think?" Chloe asked. "Does this just scream 'Train Wreck, here I come'?"

"I'm not sure," Riley said. "If it's short enough, yes. If it's not, it's more like 'receptionist in dentist's office'."

"Ick." Chloe jammed the dress back on to the rack really fast. "I'll keep looking."

Riley wandered towards the back wall, where all the pants were hanging.

"Riley?" a woman's voice called from behind her.

Riley whirled around but didn't see anyone. Weird, she thought. I don't shop here *that* often. Do the salesclerks know me or something?

"Riley!" This time the voice sounded slightly annoyed.

Riley scanned the store, looking towards other departments.

Finally she spotted a woman coming towards her.

Oh, no! It was Sierra's mom!

"Hi," Mrs. Pomeroy said, weaving her way through the Trendsetters clothing department from the main aisle. "What are you doing here, Riley? I thought you and your sister were working with Sarah on a science fair project. Are you here alone?"

For half a second, Riley thought about lying. But she knew that Sierra could come walking out of the dressing room at any moment.

"Uh, no," Riley said. "Chloe and Sarah are here." She glanced over her shoulder. "Somewhere."

Mrs. Pomeroy frowned. "What happened to the science project?" she asked.

For a moment, Riley couldn't think straight. All she could think was: What if Sierra comes out of the dressing room in that stretchy leopard-print top? Her mother will kill her!

"Uh, we *were* working on it," Riley mumbled, trying to come up with something. "But we finished early."

"Finished?" Sierra's mom sounded excited.

"No! I mean, we couldn't do any more tonight because we ran out of supplies," Riley babbled.

Sierra's mom wasn't buying it. She glanced around the Trendsetters department. "Supplies? Like what?" she said sarcastically. "Skirts and jeans? And where is Sarah, anyway?"

Oh, no, Riley thought. *Don't* go looking for her – please!

"I'll get her," Riley said, racing towards the dressing room. "Wait here. I know where she is."

Just as Riley bolted into the dressing room, Chloe was on her way out.

"What do you think?" Chloe asked, modelling a different little dress.

"Emergency!" Riley said, ignoring Chloe's question. "Sierra's mom is here! You've got to keep her busy until Sierra can change into – I don't know – something acceptable."

Chloe looked totally panicked, but she nodded and zoomed out to the main part of the floor.

"Sierra?" Riley called, peeking under all the dressing-room doors.

"In here," Sierra answered.

Riley found her and explained the problem.

"I'm dead," Sierra said, gazing at the clothes she had worn to the mall.

Riley checked them out quickly. Hanging on the back of the dressing-room door was Sierra's sheer blue flower-print blouse, along with her tightest black leather jeans.

"What am I going to do?" Sierra moaned. "If she catches me in this, I'll never see daylight again."

"Wait right here," Riley said. "The Prep Shop is right across the aisle. I'll get you something really conservative to wear. Don't worry, I'll be right back!"

Riley ran out of the dressing room and instantly ducked down, below the level of the clothing racks, so

Mrs. Pomeroy wouldn't see her. She sneaked into the next department.

Let's see. Tartan should work, Riley thought. That's preppy enough. And navy blue. Mothers always like navy blue.

She grabbed the clothes and started back to the dressing room. But halfway there, she froze. Mrs. Pomeroy was pushing past Chloe, trying to go and find Sierra herself!

In a total panic, Riley zoomed around to the other side of the department. Luckily, Riley had noticed another entrance to the dressing room at the back.

"Here. Put these on – quick!" she told Sierra. Then she headed Mrs. Pomeroy off at the other entrance. "She'll be right out," Riley explained. "Wait till you see what she's trying on. You're going to love it."

The tight-lipped smile on Sierra's mom didn't look good. But it didn't look too bad.

While they waited for Sierra, Chloe kept chattering away.

"For a while, we thought maybe we'd do a chemistry experiment for the science fair project," Chloe said.

"Really? Tell me about it," Mrs. Pomeroy said.

"Uh, well, you know… chemistry," Chloe said.

She shot Riley a pleading "help me out here" glance.

"Sure," Riley jumped in. "You know – like what kind of chemistry does it take between a guy and a girl to make them have a good time at the prom? Or something like that. It was going to be a complete survey – in the *social* sciences."

Sierra's mom started tapping her foot.

I'm getting that unhappy-mom vibe, Riley thought. Big time.

"So what *is* this project about?" Mrs. Pomeroy asked.

What is it? Yikes! Riley and Chloe hadn't come up with a good story for that yet.

Just in time, Sierra popped out of the dressing room in the tartan skirt and navy sweater.

She had her hair brushed straight and tied up in a ponytail, the way her mother liked it, too.

Smart, Riley thought. I wonder where she found a scrunchie?

Then she noticed that Sierra had used a plastic price tag thing to hold her hair back.

"Hi, Mom!" she said cheerfully. "What do you think?"

She modelled the outfit.

"I tried to get you to buy that last week," her mother said. "And you refused."

Oops!

"Uh, well, *we* were trying to pressure her into buying it, too," Riley said, talking fast. "See? And parents say peer pressure is a bad thing."

Mrs. Pomeroy shook her head. "I don't know what's going on here," she said. "But I'm really disappointed in you, Sarah. You're not working on your science fair project at all. Every time I see you, you're doing something else."

"No, Mom, that's not true," Sierra argued.

"Yes, it is," Mrs. Pomeroy insisted. "And I'm beginning to think you're just using it as an excuse to get out of the violin competition on Saturday."

"No way!" Sierra protested. "I'd never do that. You *know* I love violin."

Her mother squinted her eyes. "You do?" She was obviously testing her daughter.

"Definitely," Sierra said, and Riley knew it was true.

"Well, good," her mother said. "Then you'd better go home and start practising right now – because you're going to that competition on Saturday. And that's final." Then she turned and walked away.

Oh, no, Riley thought. We let Sierra down again! She turned to Chloe. "What are we going to do?"

"Nothing," Sierra answered for her. "Forget it. I'll never get her to change her mind now. I might as well kiss my big chance on the radio goodbye."

chapter eight

Chloe twisted a strand of her hair around her finger the next day at lunch.

"Think!" she begged Amanda. "There's got to be *something* we can do to help Sierra."

"I don't even know her," Amanda said. "Do you think her mom would buy it if she just said, 'Mom, I can't play the violin on Saturday because I want to be a rock star instead'?"

"Nope. No way," Chloe said. "Not according to Sierra, anyway."

She took a bite of her fruit salad and decided to shift gears. It was Thursday already, and the weekend was looking like a disaster.

If she was going to the Train Wreck, she had to find out who Rafe was – and soon!

"Okay, maybe you can help me with this," Chloe said. She passed one of the flyers to Amanda across the lunch table. "The flyer says 'Ask Rafe'. Maybe it's a code. Or a riddle or a tricky clue."

"I think it's a clue, all right," Amanda said. "It's a clue that means you've got to know who Rafe is."

"You're no help," Chloe complained, stabbing her fork into another piece of fruit.

"Okay," Amanda said, sipping her Coke. "Let me think." She stared at the flyer for a minute. "Maybe it's a phone number," she said finally. "Like in those ads on TV. You know, 1-800-ASK-RAFE."

Chloe laughed. "That's what Sierra said, too."

"Really? Well, did you call it?" Amanda asked.

Chloe shook her head. "No, I thought she was just kidding."

Amanda reached into her bag and pulled out her phone. "It's worth a try," she said. "Go ahead." She passed the phone to Chloe.

Why not? Chloe thought. Wouldn't it be cool if it worked? She dialled the number and waited while it rang.

"Thank you for calling the Royal Academy for Feline Excellence," a computer voice said. "If you are calling to enroll your cat in RAFE, press one. If your cat is already a student at RAFE, press two."

Chloe burst out laughing and handed the phone back to Amanda. "Hit redial," she said. "You've got to hear this!"

Amanda giggled while she listened. "Should we sign up Andrea?" she suggested."What do you think?"

"Oooh, meow," Chloe said. "With a catty remark like that, maybe we should sign *you* up!"

Amanda blushed, and Chloe knew why. She didn't usually make mean comments about other people. That's what Chloe liked about Amanda. She was really straightforward and nice.

"I just think Andrea should be nicer to you, since you tried to lend her your sweater and everything," Amanda explained.

"I know," Chloe agreed. "But honestly, if I were invited to the party and *she* wasn't? I'm not sure I'd risk getting Dan Harrington mad at me just so another freshman could come. Especially if that person wasn't a good friend of mine."

"True," Amanda agreed. "Me neither."

Still, Chloe thought. She wished she could talk Andrea into changing her mind!

Just then Riley dashed into the cafeteria, sat down beside Chloe and started picking at her sister's fruit salad.

"I'm starved," she said. "I was studying for a test during my free period, but I can't wait to eat. What's up?"

"Same old same old," Chloe said. "Still trying to figure out who Rafe is."

"Oh! That reminds me!" Riley said. "I overheard some seniors talking about the party in the library. It sounds like it's going to be so much fun! But anyway, from what they were saying, I don't think Rafe goes to this school any more. I think he might have graduated."

Hmm, Chloe thought. "So he could be anyone? Anyone in all of Malibu?" she said. "That's going to make him hard to find."

"Why don't you talk to Andrea again in maths class?" Riley suggested. "I mean, it's the only way."

"Okay," Chloe agreed.

Riley popped a piece of melon into her mouth with her fingers and then they all stood up to leave. Lunch was over.

"Good luck," Amanda said. "And don't worry. If Andrea doesn't cave in, you can always come over to my house on Saturday night — for a game of Old Maid!"

Chloe hurried to maths class and then hung around near the door, talking to Ethan Fong about an article he wrote in the school newspaper. Ethan was a maths whiz and a funny guy. His article was a humour piece about the statistical likelihood that West Malibu High would win a football game this year.

According to Ethan, there was zero chance.

The whole football team was ready to strangle him.

"Well, I thought it was funny," Chloe insisted.

"Thanks," Ethan said. "Hey, maybe you should join the team. They'd have a better chance of winning with you there."

Finally Andrea showed up, and Chloe casually dashed inside.

[Chloe: Have I ever told you about Mr. MacManus's maths class? The good thing about it is that he lets us sit wherever we want. So of course everyone sits in a different seat every day, depending on who they're friends with – or who they're trying to flirt with. So the trick is to make sure I sit near Andrea without making it look too obvious. Wish me luck!]

"Hi," Chloe said, slipping into a seat next to Andrea. "What's new?"

Andrea shook her head and pulled out the maths homework. Her paper was practically blank. "Nothing," she said. "Except I couldn't get these algebra problems." She leaned over her maths book.

"Oh, they weren't so bad," Chloe said. "And besides, they're not due till tomorrow. So anyway, can I ask you something?"

Andrea looked up from the homework. "What?"

"Is there *any* chance I can talk you into telling me where the Train Wreck is?" Chloe pleaded.

"I can't think about the party right now," Andrea said, annoyed. "If I flunk maths, I won't be going anywhere. I'll be grounded for life!"

Chloe checked out the expression on Andrea's face. The girl was in total panic mode. Not a good time to push for a party invitation.

The bell rang for class to start. Mr. MacManus was still standing in the doorway talking to another teacher about something, but he'd probably be finished any minute.

All at once, Chloe got a brilliant idea. "Hey, you know what?" she said. "I tutor sometimes. Maybe I could help you with your maths homework."

"Really?" Andrea looked psyched. "Could you do it today after school?"

"Definitely!" Chloe said.

"Okay," Andrea said. "Meet me at the front door after last period. We'll go to your house. Cool."

"Cool," Chloe agreed, smiling inside.

When class was over, Chloe ran to Riley's locker to tell her the good news. "I'm tutoring Andrea in maths after school!" she announced.

Riley frowned. "But you don't tutor maths. You tutor history and English."

"Don't worry. It's just easy algebra," Chloe explained. "Anyway, you're missing the whole point. If she's really grateful to me, maybe she'll give in and tell us where the party is!"

"Let's hope so," Riley said. "Because I've already told Alex I couldn't go out on Saturday night. And this is Thursday. We're totally running out of time."

"I know," Chloe admitted.

"And I hate to tell you what we'll be doing if we *don't* go to that party," Riley reminded her.

"What?" Chloe asked.

"Three words," Riley said with a sigh"'Kids… eat… free'."

chapter nine

"**Y**ou want something to drink? We've got kiwi juice," Chloe offered Andrea.

Andrea dropped her books on the couch and shook her head. "Who drinks kiwi juice?" she muttered.

"Nobody," Chloe agreed. "But it isn't bad if you add a ton of sugar and some club soda."

"No thanks." Andrea twisted a strand of dark brown hair around her finger. "Let's just do this, okay?"

"Sure," Chloe said, grabbing some crackers and a drink for herself.

She plopped down on the sofa beside Andrea and opened her maths book. "This is easy," Chloe said. "You just have to remember that whatever you do to one side of the equation, you have to do the same thing to the other side."

"Yeah, I've heard," Andrea said. She gazed around the living room.

She isn't even paying attention, Chloe thought.

"Nice poster," Andrea said, nodding towards a framed picture of a model walking down a catwalk. "Is your mom into fashion or something?"

"She's a designer," Chloe said. "She and my dad used to work together, but now he just hangs out at the beach and my mom runs the business."

"Cool," Andrea said. "Hey, who's that?"

Chloe whirled around to look behind her. Larry was standing outside on the deck again, pressing his nose to the glass.

"It's Larry," Chloe said. "Just ignore him."

"He'll go away?" Andrea asked.

"No. He'll come in anyway," Chloe explained.

A moment later, Larry opened the sliding glass door and walked in. "Hi," he said, helping himself to an apple. "So what's up?"

"Riley's not here," Chloe explained. "She's out with Alex."

"Well, I didn't come to see Riley," Larry replied.

"You didn't?" Chloe was shocked.

This was a first. Larry was always dropping in to hang around Riley. He never came for anything else.

"Nope." Larry smiled. "I came to see you – and to meet your new best friend."

Larry stared at Andrea as if he were waiting to be introduced. Andrea stared back at him as if he were out of his mind.

New best friend? That was ridiculous, Chloe thought. She and Andrea both knew that.

"Larry, this is Andrea Ripner," Chloe said, introducing them in a way-too-polite manner. "Andrea, this is the weirdest guy in the whole school. Like you didn't know that already."

Andrea laughed, and Larry did, too.

"Does she know about our bet?" Larry asked with a grin still on his face.

No, and I'll kill you if you mention it! Chloe thought.

"What bet?" Andrea asked, half interested, half bored.

"We don't have a bet. He's just daydreaming," Chloe said quickly. She stood up. "And speaking of dreaming, Larry, isn't it time for your nap or something? Let me show you a shortcut to your house." She took Larry's arm and led him to the front door.

"You're going to lose," he whispered once they were outside.

"Maybe so, but I haven't lost yet!" Chloe declared. "Now, get out of here and quit trying to ruin my plans!"

She hurried back into the living room and sat down beside Andrea again. Then she pulled out her own homework page.

"Let's see. Where were we?" Chloe started to say.

"Something about the equations," Andrea muttered.

"Oh, right. Okay, so look at this problem," Chloe said, pointing to it.

But right then the front door opened again. Chloe's mom bounced in, her arms loaded with bolts of fabric.

"Hi," Macy said, breezing through towards her workroom. Then she stopped and came back. "Oh, by the way, Chloe. I can't take you and Riley out to dinner Saturday night. I forgot that I've got to entertain a new client. Mind if we stick with Friday for our mother-daughter date?"

"No problem," Chloe said. "Friday's fine."

"Good," Macy said, swinging back towards her workroom. "Catch you later."

Chloe saw Andrea snicker a little when her mom mentioned the mother-daughter date.

Great! Now she knows what a loser I am – going out with my mom on Friday night! She'll never take us to the Train Wreck!

"Listen, I've got to get out of here," Andrea said, glancing at her watch. "Can we speed this up?"

"Okay," Chloe said. "Look. This is an easy one." She pointed at the first algebra problem.

Andrea grabbed Chloe's homework paper and put it down right beside her own. "Oh, just let me copy it," she said impatiently. "I'm never going to understand it anyway."

"Umm…" Chloe didn't know what to say.

She didn't want to let Andrea just *copy* her homework. But she was having a hard time explaining the maths. And besides, this might be her last chance to win Andrea over.

Her stomach sort of flip-flopped. "Okay," Chloe finally said, although Andrea was already copying the problems down. "But now you owe me big time."

"Fine," Andrea agreed.

"Really?" Chloe's face lit up. "So you'll tell us where the party is?"

Andrea dropped her pencil and sat back. "I don't know," she said, shaking her head. She looked Chloe in the eye. "I'd like to help you. Really. But Dan would kill me if I started inviting other people."

"Oh, come on," Chloe begged, trying to think of some way, *any* way to talk her into it. "How about if I got The Wave to play at the party?"

"The Wave? What's that?" Andrea asked.

"It's a band. My friend Sierra plays bass guitar in it," Chloe explained, trying hard to sell the idea. "Haven't you heard them at California Dream? They're soooo awesome!"

"Oh, yeah." Andrea nodded. "I've heard them, but—"

"I mean, they're really getting to be popular," Chloe went on. "They've even been asked to play on the air, live, at KMAL this weekend."

"Really?" Andrea looked impressed. But then she shook her head. "I don't think so. Dan already has three bands lined up. But I'll bet he would go crazy if you could bring Brian Orman to the party. Dan is so into him."

Brian Orman? He was the most popular DJ at KMAL. He was on the air every Saturday afternoon.

How am I supposed to do that? Chloe wondered. But she couldn't pass up the chance to get Andrea to invite her and Riley to the party.

"Okay," Chloe said quickly. "Yeah, I'll get him to come with us. So where's the party?"

"I'll talk to Dan tonight," Andrea replied. "I'll have him call you. He'll tell you how to find Rafe."

"Great!" Chloe said. "Thanks!"

"Okay, okay," Andrea said. "But just remember: You've got to bring Brian Orman to the party. That's the deal."

"For sure," Chloe promised.

Then she remembered: Sierra wasn't even *going* to the radio station on Saturday. Her mom wouldn't let her!

So there was no possible way Chloe was going to meet Brian Orman, let alone invite him to the party!

Chloe's stomach did another flip-flop. Oh, man, she thought. What have I got myself into now?

chapter
ten

"**I** am in so much trouble," Chloe moaned to Riley later that night. The two of them were huddled in their room. It was the first chance they'd had to talk since Riley'd come home that afternoon.

"What's wrong?" Riley asked. "I saw your face all through dinner. You looked like you were going to explode."

Chloe paced back and forth nervously.

"You want the good news first or the bad news?" she asked Riley.

"Give me the good," Riley said.

"We can go to the Train Wreck," Chloe said.

Uh-oh, Riley thought. Something told her that if this was the good news, the bad news was going to be *really* bad.

"That's great! What's the problem?" she asked.

"You're not going to believe this, but I promised to bring Brian Orman to the party," Chloe explained.

Riley's mouth dropped open. "How could you? We don't even know him! And we're not going to meet him, either. Sierra's mom won't let her go to the radio station on Saturday."

"I know, but she just *has* to go," Chloe said. "We've *got* to get Sierra's mom to change her mind."

"It's too late," Riley said, grabbing the phone. "Sierra told me she was going to call KMAL tonight and cancel."

"Oh, no! You've got to stop her!" Chloe said.

"I'll try." Riley punched in Sierra's number and crossed her fingers. "Hurry up, Sierra. Answer," she muttered.

The phone rang four times.

"Sometimes her mom won't even let her come to the phone when she's practising her violin," Riley whispered to Chloe.

Five rings. Finally Sierra picked up.

"Hi," Riley said. "It's me."

"Oh, Riley, I'm on the other line, talking to KMAL. Can I call you back?"

"No!" Riley said. "I mean, did you tell them you can't come to the radio station on Saturday?"

"I was just about to," Sierra said glumly.

"No, no, don't! Listen, hang up and say you'll call them back! I have to talk to you," Riley said.

"Why?" Sierra asked.

"I'll explain in a minute," Riley said. "Just do it!"

Riley waited while Sierra got rid of the person at

KMAL. It took a few minutes. Finally she came back on the line.

"What's up?" Sierra asked.

Riley quickly explained the situation to Sierra. About how they really wanted Sierra to do the radio gig for her own sake – *and* because Chloe had promised to bring Brian Orman to the big senior party.

"It's not happening," Sierra said. "I tried to talk my mom into letting me skip the violin competition on Saturday. But she won't listen. She doesn't believe we've been putting much effort into the science fair project."

Well, that's obvious, Riley thought. Too obvious.

"She demanded to see what we've done on the project so far," Sierra went on.

"Uh-oh," Riley said.

"Right. We have zip. I tried to stall. I told her it wasn't ready yet. But she didn't buy it. She said I had to choose: either I go to the violin competition or give up my lessons."

That's not fair! Riley thought. Sierra loved playing the violin, and she was really good at it. She just wanted to be able to do other things, too.

Like be in a rock band. What was wrong with that?

"Don't cancel with KMAL," Riley said. "I have an idea."

"What is it?" Sierra's voice perked up.

"What if we came up with a fantastic science fair project to show your mom? Would she change her mind and let you spend Saturday working on it some more?" Riley asked.

"I think so," Sierra said. "But how are we going to do that? We have less than twenty-four hours."

"Leave it to me," Riley said. "Just don't cancel!"

"Okay," Sierra said. "Bye."

Riley hung up and paced her room, thinking. Chloe stared at her, holding her breath. Finally Riley turned to her sister.

"How badly do you want to go to this party on Saturday night?" she asked.

Chloe threw her arms open wide, gesturing towards their closet.

"You can borrow *anything*," she said. "Anything I own!" She yanked her favourite short black skirt off the rack. "Here – take it. It's yours!"

"No, no," Riley said. "I don't want your clothes. I'm trying to decide whether I'm willing to lower myself to asking Larry for a favour."

"Do it!" Chloe said immediately. "Lower yourself! You'll be glad you did!"

Riley knew her sister was just kidding. But this was a crisis. And she could see how important it was to Chloe to make it come out right.

For that matter, Riley pretty much had her heart set on going to the Train Wreck, too.

"What's your idea?" Chloe demanded. "I can see on your face, you have a plan."

"Follow me," Riley said.

Riley and Chloe marched next door to Larry's house. Quickly Riley explained to him about how

Sierra wanted to do the radio station gig on Saturday. And how they needed a really good science fair project so that Sierra's mom would let her skip the violin competition.

"So I was wondering," Riley said slowly. "Remember that science fair thing you did in junior high? On high-voltage charges?"

Larry's face spread into a huge grin. "Riley, you remembered that?" he said. "That must be a sign: you really do like me."

[Riley: He thinks I remember that project because I like him? How about I remember it for the same reason everyone else in the whole school remembers it – because he accidentally shocked himself with a battery and two wires, and he liked it! Sometimes he can be soooo weird.]

"Do you have it?" Riley asked.

"Yeah, I think my mom put the poster-board part in the attic," Larry said.

"That's what I thought," Riley said. "Our mom saves every scrap of paper we ever doodled on."

"Yeah," Chloe agreed. "You should see the cartons of drawings she has in her closet."

"So anyway, can we borrow it?" Riley asked. She swallowed hard before saying the next part. "It would mean a lot to me."

Larry's face got all mushy-lovesick-happy. "For

79

you, Riley, my darling… anything!" he said.

He trotted up to his attic and came back with a big white display board folded in three sections. It was a little dusty, and some of the illustrations were coming unglued. But it didn't look bad – not bad at all.

"Thank you!" Chloe screamed, impulsively throwing her arms around Larry and kissing him on the cheek.

Larry's face froze. "Wait a minute," he said suspiciously. "What's going on? How come this is so important to *Chloe*?"

Uh-oh. Riley hesitated. Should she tell him the truth? That in a roundabout way he was helping them get invited to the Train Wreck?

Yeah, she had to. It wouldn't be right to lie to him. Even if she didn't like Larry as a boyfriend, he was a really good friend friend.

"If Sierra goes to KMAL on Saturday, then we can meet Brian Orman," Riley confessed. "We have to invite him to the Train Wreck – and in return, Andrea is getting us into the party."

Larry sort of sputtered. "So, you mean I'm lending you my high-voltage charges project – and because of that, I'm going to lose the bet?"

"That's pretty much it in a nutshell," Chloe admitted.

For a moment, Larry looked as if he might take the display boards back. But then he just gave Riley another one of those lovesick puppy-dog looks.

"Okay," he said with a shrug, grinning at her happily.

"Thanks!" Riley said, giving him a big grin.

"And I'll tell you what," Chloe offered. "Since you're helping me win the bet, we'll bake you a batch of blond brownies anyway."

"Deal," Larry said.

Riley and Chloe hurried back to their house. It took about an hour to make Larry's project look good enough to impress Sierra's mom. Chloe went to work retyping most of Larry's report, while Riley fixed up the illustrations with markers and coloured paper.

Then they hurried over to Sierra's house.

"Hi, Mrs. Pomeroy," Riley said when her mom answered the door. "Can we come in?"

Riley was standing there, holding the big display board. It was almost as big as she was.

Mrs. Pomeroy looked surprised. "Sure! Come in! Sarah didn't tell me you were coming."

Sierra came padding down the steps in a pair of boring corduroy jeans and a plain navy blue sweatshirt. Her hair was neatly tied back in a ponytail.

"Hey," Sierra greeted them.

"Hi," Chloe and Riley said.

Riley turned to Sierra's mom. "We wanted you to see how much work we've put into this project," she said. "Especially Sarah. She did a lot of it."

"But we aren't finished with the report yet." Chloe picked up the sales pitch. "Neither of us did the research, so we can't really finish it without her. We still have to make the model of it, too."

"Yeah," Riley jumped back in. "I mean, we can't turn it in half finished, can we? I don't know, it just doesn't seem right for Sarah to have to drop out when we're so close to being done."

They stared at Sierra's mom with big, pleading, guilt-provoking eyes. Riley held her breath. Had they laid it on too thick?

"Wow," her mother said. "I'll have to admit, I'm impressed. And a little embarrassed. I guess I didn't give you girls enough credit."

"So we can work on it on Saturday?" Chloe cheered, almost ready to hug Mrs. Pomeroy.

Whoa, girl. Calm down! Riley thought. Chloe was practically jumping for joy.

And *no one* would believe she was *that* excited about a stupid science fair project.

Except maybe Sierra's mom.

"Yes, yes, of course," her mother said, beaming. "It sounds like it's really important to all of you, so go ahead. You can even settle in here and work on it tonight at our dining table."

Whoops. Not part of the plan! Riley thought. "Actually, we left all the research stuff at our house," she mumbled quickly. "So maybe we'll just finish it this weekend."

"Okay," Mrs. Pomeroy said, sounding disappointed that she wouldn't get to watch them work.

Sierra walked them to the door and waited till her mom was out of earshot.

"You guys are the best!" she said, giving Riley a hug. "Thank you, thank you, thank you!"

"No problem," Riley said.

But in her heart, Riley knew that wasn't true.

Their problems were just beginning. Because now they still had to convince Brian Orman – a totally cool college guy – to come with them to a high-school party.

And what were the chances of that?

chapter
eleven

"**D**on't worry, he'll call you," Andrea promised Chloe the next morning in the hall at school.

The first bell hadn't rung yet, but Chloe, Riley and Andrea were trying to get to their lockers. They pushed through a crowd of people lined up to buy brownies from a chorus fund-raiser.

"But this is Friday," Chloe said. "The party's tomorrow night."

"Oh, and did I tell you?" Andrea added quickly. "It doesn't start till midnight."

Midnight? Chloe glanced at her sister. Wow. That's really late, she thought. Cool!

"So when is Dan going to call us?" Chloe asked. "I mean, we don't even know who Rafe is. And what's the usual question?"

"I'm not allowed to tell you," Andrea answered. "Just wait for Dan's call. He'll probably call you after school."

"Okay." Chloe gave in. What choice did she have?

"See you tomorrow night," Andrea called as she turned down a small hallway towards her locker.

Chloe glanced at Riley and saw a certain look on her face. "What?" she asked.

"Midnight?" Riley said. "Hello! How are we going to sneak out of the house that late?"

"Quietly?" Chloe said with a weak smile.

Riley rolled her eyes. "What if we get caught?" she said. "And I mean, we don't even know where this party is. How are we going to get there? And how will we get home? Maybe we're trying to spice up our lives *too* much."

"Look," Chloe said, exasperated. She turned to face her sister with an I-mean-business look. "We can't worry about that stuff now. We'll just play it by ear. One step at a time. It'll all work out fine. Take my word for it. Okay?"

She didn't give Riley a chance to argue. She grabbed her books from her locker and hurried to homeroom.

It seemed like forever until school was over. But finally the last bell rang.

Chloe and Riley raced home to wait for Dan's call.

"My two little peaches," Manuelo said when they walked in the door. "How's life? Spicy enough these days?"

"A few days ago we were pineapples," Riley mumbled.

"I draw the line when he starts calling us water-melons," Chloe said under her breath.

"Hey, Manuelo. Any calls for us?" Riley asked.

Manuelo's eyes seemed to sparkle. "Oh, I don't know," he said in his singsong voice. "Why don't you check the answering machine?"

"Really?" Chloe's face lit up. Someone must have called! she thought. Then she thought of something else. What if Manuelo heard it? And heard about the party?

She shot Riley a worried glance, and instantly the two of them raced to the machine.

Manuelo followed, hovering a few feet away. "Is there a new message?" he asked eagerly.

"Yes," Riley said, pushing the button to play it.

But there was only silence. Then a *click*. It was a hang-up.

Chloe's face fell. "Bummer," she said. "I wonder who that was?"

"Oh, dear." Manuelo sounded just as disappointed.

Chloe checked out his face. He was holding something back, she could tell. "Manuelo, what happened?" she asked.

"I don't know," he said. "I didn't do anything. Except—"

"Except what?" Riley demanded.

"Maybe it's the new outgoing message?" Manuelo guessed.

"*What* new message?" Riley said.

With a sheepish expression, Manuelo pushed the button to play it.

"Hello," his voice said on the machine. "You have reached the two cutest twins in Malibu. Please leave us a message. Bye-bye!"

"Oh my gosh!" Riley said, covering her face in embarrassment. "You didn't even give our names!"

"He didn't have to," Chloe said. "How many twins are there in Malibu? Everyone will know that was us!" She was totally mortified.

"Do you think Dan called, and heard that, and hung up?" Riley wondered out loud.

That's my worst fear, Chloe thought. So the answer is probably yes!

She checked caller ID. "Yup! It was Dan," she said.

"Manuelo, why did you change our message?" Riley asked as nicely as she could.

"I thought a nice, spicy message would help get you out of your rut," Manuelo admitted. "It always helps me."

Chloe put her hands together, pleading with him. "Please – no more surprises to spice up our lives, okay?" she begged.

"Okay," Manuelo promised. "Sorry about that."

The girls hurried up to their room for a little privacy.

"Now what?" Riley asked.

"Now we call Dan and ask him about the party," Chloe said, picking up the cordless phone.

Her heart picked up speed as she dialled Dan Harrington's number. It felt really weird to be calling a senior guy she didn't even know. But she was desperate! After all this, she wasn't going to miss out on this party, no matter what!

[<u>Chloe</u>: **So you're wondering how I got Dan's number? Well, I looked it up in the phone book three days ago. I figured I'd call him as a last resort – if I couldn't convince Andrea to get us invited to the party. Guess I needed the number anyway, huh?**]

Finally Dan answered and Chloe explained why she was calling. "Oh, you're the one who's bringing Brian Orman to the party?" he said.

"Uh-huh," Chloe said.

She tried to sound positive. But in the back of her mind she was thinking: How are we ever going to get him to come?

Dan could hear the uncertainty in her voice. "Is this definite?" he asked. "Andrea said you were bringing him."

"We are!" Chloe insisted. "Don't worry. He'll be there."

"He'd better be. I mean, I told everyone he's coming, and I don't want to look like an idiot," Dan said firmly.

"Don't worry," Chloe reassured him five more times.

At last Dan stopped grilling her about it. "Okay, here's the story," he said. "Every week the party's in a different place. So what you do is you go into the Swedish bakery on Saturday afternoon and ask for Rafe. He works there."

"Who's Rafe?" Chloe blurted out, interrupting him.

She'd been waiting all week to find out, and the mystery was killing her!

Dan sighed, as if he didn't want to waste time with those details. "He's just a guy who graduated from West Malibu a few years ago," he explained. "He used to run the Train Wreck, and he still helps put it together."

"Really? Even if he doesn't come?" Chloe asked.

Another sigh from Dan. "He *does* come," he said. "He's a totally cool dude."

Wow. This party was *definitely* an older crowd, Chloe realised.

"Anyway, go to the bakery and ask Rafe for a pickle Danish," Dan explained.

"There's no such thing," Chloe blurted out. At least she hoped not!

"I know," Dan said, getting really impatient. "It's just a code – so that Rafe knows you're on the party list. He'll give you a piece of paper with an address written on it. That's where the party will be. And it starts at midnight."

"Cool!" Chloe said.

"Yeah," Dan agreed.

"Okay, thanks," Chloe said.

"See you tomorrow night." Dan added, "With Brian."

"Right." Chloe hung up the phone. She turned to Riley with a huge smile on her face, then started dancing with her around the room. "I can't believe it!" she cheered. "We're going to the Train Wreck!"

chapter
twelve

Riley held her hands tightly against her ears. The music was so loud, she couldn't talk or hear a thing Chloe was saying. And the bass was booming so much, it almost hurt. But she didn't care.

This was awesome! The Wave was playing live, on the air, at KMAL.

And Riley and Chloe were in the studio with them!

They stood against the wall, crammed into a space behind some amps, microphone stands and cables.

Sierra looked amazing in a black lace blouse with black jeans. Her red hair was flowing all over the place as she played. And Alex was singing a song he'd written for Riley. Every once in a while, he'd glance up from his guitar and their eyes would meet.

Brian Orman, the DJ, was banging his head wildly to the music. He had sun-bleached wavy hair, kind of long, like a surfer. His heather-grey T-shirt said "KMAL" in silver letters across his chest.

He's totally into Sierra's band, Riley thought. This was the best! During a break he'd even asked The Wave to come back and play again another time.

Oh, man, Riley thought with a laugh. If that happens, Sierra will have to come up with something better than a science fair project as a cover-up!

When the song was over, the band took another break.

"Now's our chance," Chloe whispered to Riley.

Yeah, Riley thought. They had to do it sometime.

She and Chloe waited till Brian had finished announcing the next CD. Then they went up to him.

"Uh, can we talk to you?" Riley asked.

"Sure. What's up?" he said, giving them a sweet grin.

"Well, it's sort of a favour," Chloe hedged, glancing at Riley for support.

"Spit it out," he said, still smiling encouragingly.

Okay. Here goes, Riley thought. "Some friends of ours are having a party tonight," Riley said. "It's sort of a weekly party, in a warehouse somewhere. Anyway, we were wondering if you wanted to come along."

Brian grinned even wider. "To the Train Wreck? Sure, why not? Where is it this week?" he said.

Riley blinked in surprise. "You've heard of it?"

"Of course," Brian said. "The Train Wreck is legendary. I used to go when Rafe was in charge. He was the man in the old days. I'll tell you — some of those nights were unbelievable. I mean, stuff happens, you know? Stuff you *never* forget."

Riley swallowed hard. Stuff happens? What kind of stuff? she wondered. She shot a worried glance at Chloe, but Chloe didn't react.

"So you'll come?" Chloe asked.

"Just name the time and place," Brian said. "Me and my buds will be there."

Wow, Riley thought. He's bringing his friends, too? This was *really* going to be an older crowd.

"It doesn't start till midnight," Chloe said. "And we've got to find out the location from Rafe."

"Oh, right." Brian nodded. "So do you want me to pick you guys up?"

"Pick us up? You mean in a car?" Riley asked.

It was bad enough that they were planning to sneak out at midnight. But going in a car with a guy who was at least five years older than they were?

Mom would have a fit if she ever found out, Riley thought. She shot Chloe another worried glance.

"Um, I don't know," Chloe said. "I'm not sure how we're getting there."

That was the trouble, Riley realised. If they *didn't* go with Brian, how *would* they get to the party?

"I guess you could pick us up," Riley said. "Thanks." She wrote down their address on a piece of paper. "But don't ring the bell," she told Brian. "And don't blow the horn. I don't want you to wake my mom."

"Right," Chloe chimed in. "Just park outside and we'll come out."

"Okay," Brian said. "See you at midnight."

Riley checked her watch. "We've got to hurry, if we're going to get to the Swedish bakery," she told her sister.

"Let's go." Chloe grabbed her sweater.

They gave Sierra a hug and congratulated her on a great performance. Then Riley said goodbye to Alex.

"Be careful at that party tonight," he said. "Are you sure you want to go?"

I *did* want to, Riley thought. But now she wasn't so sure. Still, she couldn't back out now.

"I have to," Riley whispered. "Chloe's counting on it."

"Well, call me tomorrow," he said.

"I will," Riley promised.

Then she and Chloe zoomed to catch the bus.

Twenty minutes later, they walked into the Swedish bakery. The store was busy. Two older women were ahead of them. So was a father with a small child.

Finally they got to the front counter. An old man with white hair gave them a toothy smile. "What can I do for you ladies?" he asked.

"Um, we came to see Rafe," Riley said.

"Oh." The old man shook his head in disgust. "He hasn't come in yet. And would you look at this?" He gestured towards the clock. "We're going to close up in an hour!"

"He hasn't come in?" Chloe repeated.

"Nope. Can I get you something?" the man asked.

Chloe looked at Riley desperately.

"Um, do you have a pickle Danish by any chance?" Riley blurted out.

"Sure!" the old man said. He reached behind him to a rack of baked goods, and pulled a pastry off the shelf. "How many do you want?"

"Just one," Riley said, staring at it in disgust.

Yuk! she thought. It looked gross. It was like a fruit Danish, only there were chopped up pickles on top!

"You're the tenth person today who's asked for a pickle Danish," the owner explained. "So I made some!"

"Oh," Riley said, paying him and taking the pastry in a small white bag. "Well, thanks."

"What now?" Chloe said as they walked slowly towards the door. "Don't tell me we've done all this for nothing."

Before Riley could answer, the door pushed open and a young guy with two earrings came into the bakery.

"There you are!" the old man behind the counter called. "Finally. People have been asking for you all day! What took you so long?"

"Sorry," the guy said, hurrying to put on his apron. "I had a flat tyre. Took forever to get it changed."

"Is that Rafe?" Chloe whispered to Riley.

The guy overheard her. "I'm Rafe. What do you need?"

"A pickle Danish?" Riley said, bracing herself for another gross pastry.

"Okay, yeah." Rafe reached into his jeans pocket and pulled out a small slip of paper. But he didn't hand it to

94

them. "You guys look a little young for this party," he said, eyeing them sideways. "What are you? Freshmen?"

"It's okay," Chloe said quickly, tossing her hair back and trying to look older. "Dan invited us. It's all good."

Rafe sort of shook his head, but he gave them the address. "If you say so. But be careful."

Wow, Riley thought. That's what Alex said, too.

The two of them hurried out of the door.

"Are you thinking what I'm thinking?" Riley asked once she and Chloe were alone again, outside on the sidewalk.

"What?" Chloe asked.

"This party sounds pretty wild," Riley explained. "I mean, college guys are going to be there. Are you ready for that?" Because I'm definitely not! Riley thought.

"Not exactly," Chloe admitted. "But maybe it won't be too out of control. If Andrea's going, it should be okay. Right?"

"I don't know about that." Riley thought about it. "We don't really know Andrea very well. Maybe she's a lot wilder than we are."

"Two ten-year-olds with a couple of squirt guns are a lot wilder than we are!" Chloe moaned.

"That's not true," Riley argued.

Although it might be, she thought.

"No," Chloe said firmly, as though she'd made up her mind. "We're going to this party tonight. I practically killed myself trying to get us invited. And now we finally have the address. So we're going – and that's that."

chapter
thirteen

"Uh-oh," Chloe said. "Don't look now, but I think we're being followed."

"By who?" Riley asked, glancing over her shoulder.

"I said don't look!" Chloe scolded.

The two of them were walking along the beach road towards their house.

"Who is it?" Riley asked.

A green minivan pulled up beside them and slowed down.

"Hi," Sierra's mom called from the driver's seat. "I keep running into you like this. Where's Sarah?"

Where's Sarah? She was probably still at KMAL, Chloe thought. Or hanging out with the band after the gig.

But she couldn't tell Sierra's mom that.

"We finished working on our project a while ago,"

Riley said, thinking fast. "I think she was headed home. Or maybe she went to get something to eat."

"Oh! So you finished?" Sierra's mom sounded happy. "That's great."

"Yeah," Chloe nodded. Then she noticed the radio in Mrs. Pomeroy's car. The voice of the DJ was familiar.

That's Brian Orman, Chloe thought. Her heart started thudding. Uh-oh. Sierra's mom is listening to KMAL!

"Great station," Chloe mumbled, nodding towards the car radio. "Do you, um, do you listen to it much? I mean, I thought you liked only classical music."

"Oh, I like all kinds of music," Mrs. Pomeroy said. "It's a good station. I check it out when I'm in the mood."

Chloe gulped. Had Sierra's mom heard the band? It didn't seem like it. She was pretty calm, anyway.

"Were you listening to it half an hour ago?" Chloe asked, sort of stammering.

Sierra's mother gave her a why-do-you-want-to-know look.

"We had it on for a while this afternoon while we were working on our science project," Chloe explained. "And I thought I heard a really good band. The one that was live in the studio."

Mrs. Pomeroy nodded in agreement. "They *were* good, weren't they? What was that band called? The Wave?"

"Something like that," Riley said.

Duh! Chloe thought. As if we don't know!

"Yeah, I liked them. Well, anyway, I'm glad you girls are finished," Mrs. Pomeroy said. "I'd better go. I've got ice cream and frozen food melting in the back."

Chloe backed away from the car, and Sierra's mom drove off.

"Wow," Riley said when she was gone. "Close one."

"Yeah," Chloe said. "Can you believe it? Her mom actually loved the band! Sierra should tell her the truth about it."

"I know," Riley agreed. "But I bet she won't."

When they got home, they dragged themselves up to their room to relax. Riley flopped on her bed while Chloe went through her closet, trying to decide what to wear to the party. The cute little outfit she had bought at Birch's didn't seem right somehow.

She glanced at her alarm clock on the dresser. "Only seven hours to go!" Chloe said.

Riley sighed. "I'm exhausted already."

"Hello?" Manuelo called, knocking on the door. "Can I come in?"

"Sure," Chloe said. "What's up?"

Manuelo stepped into their room, hiding something behind his back. "I know I've been messing things up for you lately," he said, sounding sorry. "Rearranging your room, changing the answering machine. So I thought I'd make it up to you. This time I have a really *good* surprise. Ta-da!"

He whipped out his hand, holding two concert tickets.

"What are those?" Riley asked.

"Tickets for a Pigeon Powder concert – tonight in L.A.!" Manuelo announced proudly.

Pigeon Powder? They were the hottest new group around. Riley and Chloe both loved their CD.

Oh, wow, that would be awesome, Chloe thought, checking out Riley's face. Her sister clearly felt the same way. It *would* be awesome – any night but tonight.

"See? I knew you'd be happy!" Manuelo said. "You're speechless!"

"Uh, that's so nice of you!" Chloe said quickly. "Except Riley and I already have plans for tonight."

"You do? What?" Manuelo's face fell.

Think of something! Chloe told herself.

"We, uh, have our hearts set on staying home to watch a TV Land marathon," Riley jumped in. "We've been planning it for weeks."

"TV Land?" Manuelo looked hurt and confused. "Ohhh. That's better than Pigeon Powder?" he asked.

"It is tonight," Chloe said, feeling really bad about hurting his feelings.

"Ohhh," Manuelo said again. He turned to leave with the tickets still in his hands. Then he turned back. "Are you sure?"

Chloe nodded. "Sorry, Manuelo, but we've just... you know... been waiting so long for this."

"Okay," he said. "If you say so. I guess I'll call a friend and go to the concert myself."

When he was gone, Chloe's shoulders sagged. "Are we nuts?" she said. "I mean, we just passed up Pigeon Powder!"

"You said it, I didn't," Riley replied with a glum look.

Finally Manuelo called them for dinner. Afterwards, the girls sprawled on the couch and watched TV Land, waiting for Manuelo to leave. Mom had already gone to the business dinner with her new client.

When Manuelo left, they had the house to themselves. They flipped to MTV until they'd seen the same five videos twice.

"It's still early," Chloe said, checking out the clock. "But I'm going to get ready."

Riley followed her. "Me, too."

Chloe went through her closet and changed her clothes four times. She finally settled on a pair of black- and-red checked hip-huggers and a short black sweater.

After all, she decided, this party was in a warehouse somewhere. She didn't want to be *too* dressed up. Then she did her hair, using a curling iron to get the waves just right.

Riley put on a camisole with a sheer green top over it, and green jeans to match.

"Now what?" Riley asked after she'd finished brushing her hair for the tenth time. "It's only ten o'clock."

Chloe listened. "Oops. Mom's home," she said, hearing the front door open and close. Quickly she went over to their dresser and flipped off the light.

"Why'd you do that?" Riley asked softly.

"So she'll think we're asleep," Chloe whispered. "Otherwise, if she comes up here and sees us all dressed to go out, she'll know something's up."

"Oh," Riley whispered back in the dark.

Chloe felt her way to her bed. "Where are you, Riley?" she asked quietly.

"Sitting on the end of my bed," Riley replied.

"Me, too," Chloe said.

For ten minutes, the girls sat there, not saying a word.

Chloe yawned. "I'm so sleepy," she said.

"Tell me about it," Riley agreed.

"I'm going to take a nap," Chloe said. "Just for twenty minutes. You stay awake while I sleep, and then we'll trade off."

"Okay," Riley whispered.

Chloe lay back on her bed, her legs dangling off the end. She closed her eyes.

Just a quick nap, she thought.

And then I'll be ready to paaaar-ty!

chapter
fourteen

Riley opened her eyes. Something jerked her out of her dream. Was someone knocking? At the window?

She tried to look, then winced.

Ouch. The sun was so bright, so blindingly bright. She squinted, covering her eyes.

"What time is it?" she said, sitting up groggily and looking at her clock.

"Huh?" Chloe woke up slowly beside her.

"Riley? Can I come in?" the voice at the window said.

Riley rubbed her eyes and sat up.

It took a minute for her to figure out where they were, and why. Then it hit her.

"Oh, no!" she blurted out. "Chloe! Wake up! We slept through the party!"

Chloe bolted upright. "What time is it? What happened? You're kidding!" she screamed.

"Nope," Riley said. "Look at us!"

Both girls were still dressed in the clothes they had put on last night. Still lying on top of their made beds.

"We fell asleep and missed it!" Riley said.

"Oh, no," Chloe moaned. "I don't believe it. Larry will never let me forget this. After all that, we still didn't go to the party!"

"Riley!" the voice called, still knocking at the window.

"And there he is now," Riley said, stretching and stumbling out of bed.

She straightened her wrinkled green top and fluffed her bed hair. Then she went to the window and opened it.

Larry was outside their window. On a ladder. As usual.

"Hi," he said, grinning at her. "You look so beautiful when your hair resembles a rat's nest."

"Larry, what are you doing here?" Riley asked.

"I came to tell you about the party," Larry said as he climbed in through the window.

"What about it?" Riley asked.

"And how would you know, anyway?" Chloe asked, still yawning and sleepy.

"I was worried about you," he said to Riley. "So I went to the party – just to make sure you guys were okay."

That was sweet, Riley thought. Sort of annoying, and macho, and overly protective – but sweet.

"No way," Chloe said. "How did you get the address?"

"From Rafe," Larry said. "And, um, yum. I *love* pickle Danish."

Of course! Riley thought. Typical Larry.

"So what happened?" Chloe grilled him. "Tell us everything!"

"It was totally out of control," Larry said. "The police even raided the place. I had to get out of there fast, to avoid being arrested."

"Are you serious?" Chloe's eyes were wide.

Larry nodded. "And guess what else?" His smile danced, teasing them.

"What?" Riley held her breath.

"Brian Orman never showed. He just blew it off," Larry said.

"Maybe," Riley said. "Or maybe he waited for us outside forever and then finally gave up when we never came out of the house."

"Whoa," Larry said. "You mean you didn't even *try* to get there? I wondered why you didn't show. I figured your mom caught you or something."

"We fell asleep," Riley admitted. "But don't you dare tell anyone!"

Larry crossed his heart. "Would I ever betray you, Riley, my darling?"

"Oh, man, this is bad," Chloe said. "We look like idiots to Dan Harrington now."

"Not necessarily," Larry said.

"Why not?" Chloe asked.

"When you didn't show up, I sort of put the word out that you guys had a better offer," he said.

That's so sweet! Riley thought. He was always looking out for her. Even at times like this.

"Actually, we *did* have a better offer," Chloe said. "We had tickets to Pigeon Powder."

"Really?" Larry looked jealous.

"We should have gone, too," Riley said. "That would have been so much fun."

Chloe picked up a brush and started brushing her hair.

"Chloe, do me a favour," Riley said. "Promise me from now on, no more plans to spice up our lives. At least for a while. I *like* being in a rut."

"It's a deal," Chloe promised.

Manuelo called up the stairs. "Chloe! Riley! Breakfast in ten minutes! I've got your favourites: French toast, OJ, and bacon."

"Perfect!" Chloe answered. "We'll be right down!"

Riley's stomach rumbled. She couldn't wait to eat a normal breakfast again.

"Oops," Chloe said, looking at their clothes. "We'd better change before we go downstairs. Otherwise, Mom and Manuelo will know we slept in these clothes."

"Right," Riley agreed. "Larry, goodbye." She pushed him towards the window, so they could change.

105

"Okay," he said. "But I'm coming over later to collect my blond brownies. You guys promised, remember?" Then he stopped and glanced at something on Chloe's desk. "Hey, is this your maths homework?"

"So?" Chloe said.

"Is this what you let Andrea copy?" he asked.

Chloe nodded.

"Oh, boy," Larry said. "These answers are all wrong. She's going to get an F and so are you. Big time."

"Oh, no!" Chloe cried. "Andrea's going to freak!"

"Well, you've got to admit one thing, Chloe," Riley said with a smile. "At least next week won't be boring!"

"Yeah," Chloe agreed. "Tell me about it."

Chloe
and Riley's

SCRAPBOOK

so little time

Check out book 6!

secret crush

Fourteen-year-old Chloe Carlson's stomach did a little flip when her father pulled up in front of the Sunnyview Retirement Home. The place was a lot closer to home than she'd thought. And she was starting to get nervous!

"Thanks for the ride, Dad," she said. "I can walk home later." She gave her boyfriend Jake a quick kiss on the cheek, but she didn't get out of the car.

"Okay, honey." Jake waited a second. "Chloe? Aren't you going in?"

"Actually, I feel a little weird about this," Chloe admitted. "I mean, what am I going to do with these people? There's such a generation gap. We have nothing in common. What will we talk about?"

Jake smiled. "Just be yourself. Older people aren't aliens — you'll have plenty to talk about."

Like what? Chloe wondered, getting out of the car. They won't care about stuff like hot clothes or the latest mocha java frappé at Starbucks. But as she walked up to the apartment building, she gave herself a pep talk. Be positive. After all, you'll be helping somebody out. And you're getting extra credit. Community service will look great on your college application. So what if you won't be applying for another three years?

Chloe walked past two flower-filled planters and pulled open the front door.

Quinn Reyes, one of Chloe's friends from school, was sitting on one of the chairs inside the roomy lobby, talking on her mobile. Another friend, Amanda Grey, was checking out the huge bulletin board hanging on one of the walls.

Chloe waved to Quinn and hurried over to Amanda. "Hi, Amanda! I didn't know you'd signed up for this."

"I didn't know *you* had," Amanda said.

"It was sort of a last-minute thing," Chloe told her. She glanced around. Two elderly women crossed the lobby and stopped at the mailboxes on the other side of the room. A man and a woman moved slowly towards the front doors. "So what are we supposed to do?" she asked. "Just grab somebody and ask if they need anything?"

Amanda tucked her brown hair behind her ears and laughed. "Not exactly. When Mrs. Carpenter —

she's the director of Sunnyview – came to talk to us at school, she said she'd introduce us to the people who signed up for the programme. I haven't seen her yet, so I guess we wait."

Amanda headed for one of the chairs. As Chloe started to follow her, she brushed against the bulletin board. A Chinese take-away menu fluttered to the floor. Chloe grabbed it and stuck it back on.

The bulletin board was almost totally covered: more take-away menus, senior-citizen hotline numbers, bus schedules, symphony and museum brochures, and a "Sunnyview Birthday List".

As she checked out some of the notices, Chloe heard footsteps behind her. She turned.

A boy stood a couple of feet away. Grey eyes, curly dark hair and a crooked little smile that made him look like he'd just heard a private joke.

Cute, Chloe thought. Very cute. She'd seen him before. He was a transfer student at West Malibu High. She didn't know his name, but she could definitely think of a few things to say to *him*. Maybe Sunnyview had flirting potential after all!

Chloe gave herself a quick, mental once-over. Too bad she'd worn such blah clothes. But at least she had on her cute accessories – her favourite turquoise choker and hand-beaded bracelet. "Hi," she said with a smile.

"Hey," he said. He moved closer and leaned next

to the bulletin board. "I'm Brian Porter."

"Chloe Carlson," she told him. "I've seen you around school." His eyes weren't totally grey, Chloe noticed. There was blue in them, too. They looked really cool with the dark hair.

"Me, too. I mean, I've seen you." He grinned. "Actually, I've seen two of you."

Chloe laughed. "You must have seen me with Riley, my sister. We're twins."

"Right, I figured that out pretty fast," he said. "So you're Chloe," he added.

Chloe nodded. "Yup." She loved the way he kept looking at her.

"So let me guess," Brian said. "You're here to do your part as a good citizen of Malibu."

"You mean the community service thing? Right," Chloe agreed.

Brian nodded. "That's what I figured, since I haven't seen you here before."

"What do you mean? Are you visiting your grandparents or something?" Chloe asked. "I thought you were a volunteer, too."

"I am. I've been working here ever since I moved back to Malibu."

"Back?" Chloe repeated.

"Yeah," Brian said. I used to live here. When I was a kid my mom moved us to Japan for business. Then India. Then Italy..."

"Really? I'm impressed," Chloe said.

Brian shrugged. "No big deal."

"Well, I've barely been out of California," Chloe admitted. "My parents took me and my sister to the Grand Canyon once. It was cool." And so is he, she thought. Not to mention, totally hot! "So, what do you do here?" she asked, trying to sound casual.

"I do stuff for Mrs. Scanlon and Mrs. Davidson," Brian told her. "They're widows. Also cousins, and they share an apartment. It's fun. I like it."

"You do?" Chloe knew she sounded surprised, but she couldn't help it. How could spending so much time at a retirement home be fun?

Brian smiled. "A lot of kids don't like it – but they sign up because it looks good on their college applications. Don't worry," he added softly, "I won't tell anybody that's why *you're* here."

"That's... that's *not* the reason I volunteered!" Chloe sputtered, even though it kind of was. "Why did you say that?"

"Because of your outfit," he said.

"My outfit?" Chloe said. "What's the matter with it?"

He shrugged. "Nothing. Except you don't dress like that at school. It's obvious you're wearing your 'old folks' clothes. It's like you're playing a part. You aren't serious about this."

Chloe felt her cheeks burn. Who did this Brian guy think he was? Okay, so maybe she wasn't thrilled about being there. And maybe she was kind of glad to get the extra credit. But that didn't mean she couldn't be serious about volunteering. Just because he'd been all over the world didn't mean that he knew *everything*...

To be continued...